# SHERLOCK HOLMES
## and the Singular Adventure
### of

# THE GLOVED PIANIST

CW01019881

# SHERLOCK HOLMES
## and the Singular Adventure
## of
# THE GLOVED PIANIST

Alan Stockwell

SHERLOCK HOLMES
and the Singular Adventure
of
THE GLOVED PIANIST
Copyright © Alan Stockwell 2010
*All Rights Reserved*

The right of Alan Stockwell to be identified as the author
of this work has been asserted by him in accordance with
the Copyright, Designs and Patents Act 1988

ISBN 978-0-9565013-1-8

Published 2010 by
VESPER HAWK PUBLISHING

www.vesperhawk.com

www.mrsherlockholmes.co.uk

# PREFACE

My previous book *The Singular Adventures of Mr Sherlock Holmes* was a conscious attempt to emulate as closely as possible the original short stories of Sir Arthur Conan Doyle. The fiction I put forward was that the book was a final collection of Dr Watson's writings and was an extension of the Canon. To add verisimilitude to this conceit I included a spoof reprint of the obituary of Sherlock Holmes (and was taken to task by some on the grounds that "Sherlock Holmes will live forever") and a preface informing the reader that the work was a final gasp from the ailing Dr Watson.

As a firm believer that Holmes and Watson should always remain in their own time and place I did my best to provide a simulacrum of Dr Watson's style. Whether I succeeded or not is for the reader to judge.

The District Messenger – The SH Society of London
*"Mr Stockwell clearly knows his period."*

Robert Robinson – BBC Broadcaster and Author
*"You hit off the idiom with remarkable accuracy."*

Dale Harris – doyen of Amazon Reviewers
*"A wonderful collection of tales by one who has mastered the world of Sherlock Holmes."*

Alĕs Kododrubec – President of the Czech Society of SH
*"The stories look like being from the pen of John H Watson himself."*

Midwest Book Review
*"Completely faithful to the spirit and tone of the original Doyle stories."*

The Torr Journal – SH Society of the West Country.
*"Alan Stockwell has captured the style of Dr Watson very well."*

David Stuart Davies, a world authority on Sherlock Holmes, concluded his review in Sherlock Magazine with the words *"One of the best collections of Holmes pastiches for some time. Recommended."*

The present story *The Gloved Pianist* is somewhat different. It is longer than a short story but has not been stretched to contrive a novel; even the original Holmes novels do not work as well as the short stories. It is also couched in the form of a typical "whodunit" – something that Doyle never offered his readers. But be assured: I have not succumbed to the abominations of making Holmes meet Dracula, or sending him time-travelling, or into outer space. The time and place is still the world of Holmes and Watson but they are gradually aging into the beginning of the 20th century. The story is still narrated by Dr Watson and the period details are as accurate as research allows. However, the format of the "whodunit" being unnatural to the normally secretive Holmes, some liberties have been deliberately taken.

Thus on this occasion the reader is offered a work more akin to a blend of the departed spirit of Dame Agatha Christie and the shade of Sir Arthur Conan Doyle.

SHERLOCK HOLMES
and the Singular Adventure
of

THE GLOVED PIANIST


THE STORY

IT was early in the year 1905 that the unexpected disappearance of the Honourable Edward Dunstable from a locked room caused a sensation in the London press. As is now known, he turned up a mere few days later and the whole affair became something of a damp squib, but it was the talk of London for, if not nine days, at least five.

However, it is not generally known that my friend Sherlock Holmes was involved in the mystery and as it is a case which has some points of interest to the *aficionado* of crime and the student of human nature, I lay it before my readers without any apology for the apparent simplicity of the explanation for the crime. I call it a crime but, of course, it was no crime at all; merely a young man trying to escape from his father's dominance.

Mr Sherlock Holmes'ss involvement started with a telegram followed by a visit from Lord Challis, father of the Hon Edward Dunstable. We had endured a blustery night but the day was now serene until the late afternoon when we were assailed by another bout of bluster as the noble lord bustled in.

"Mr Sherlock Holmes?"

"I am he. This is my friend and confidant Dr Watson," replied Holmes.

"Good afternoon to you, Doctor. I must impress upon you, Mr Holmes, that the affair on which I earnestly seek your advice is of a personal nature and, to be frank, the fewer people involved the better."

"You can speak freely before Dr Watson, my lord. I cannot listen to anything you have to say which omits my colleague," said Holmes suavely.

"Very well, if you say so. But I do impress upon you

the rather delicate nature of what I am about to relate, as I confess it does not put my family in a very good light."

"Nothing you have to say will pass beyond these four walls, you have my assurance," replied Holmes.

"Very well. It is like this. My son and heir Edward Dunstable is prone to – well, not to put too fine a point on it – walking in his sleep."

Lord Challis paused as though this was a startling revelation that would cause us to react in a marked manner. As a medical man I, of course, was well versed in the phenomenon of somnambulism and it is usually a temporary thing brought on by a particularly stressful situation in a person's life; for Holmes'ss part, nothing in the whole world surprised him.

"He has been prone to sleepwalking ever since childhood. We had a terrible time of it when his grandmother died. He was about twelve years old at the time and his grandmother's death hit him particularly hard. They were very close. But that is all in the past. He is five-and-twenty now and a captain in the army and the whole thing has started up again. You can imagine what I feel, as his father, to realise my son is incapable of knowing what he is doing. Wandering abroad at night getting into all kinds of danger."

"I am sure your son is merely passing through some stressful period in his life that has caused this sleepwalking to reappear. It is only a medical complaint, such as influenza or a broken leg may be," I felt bound to interject.

"Pray go on, my lord, for as yet I fail to see why you require the assistance of a detective," said Holmes with a touch of asperity.

"I thank you for your comments, Dr Watson. But I cannot help thinking, perhaps, my son has a fevered brain or is unhinged in some way. Edward was out in Rooiwal in '02 and although he was in the victorious army he probably went through hell out there. He never spoke of it much but he resigned his commission. However, Mr

Holmes, as to why I have come to you. It is rather embarrassing to have to say this to strangers but – well, I have taken to locking Edward in his room each night. It is for his own good. His mother and I discussed the possibility he could well wander about the house and do some damage to himself. His mother is terrified that he might leave the house and roam around the garden, maybe fall into the pond. We really do have his best interests at heart."

"I am sure you have, my lord, but I still do not see where I am needed," said Holmes.

"He's gone, Mr Holmes. This morning when I went to unlock the door I found that he was not in the room. His bed had not been slept in and there was no trace of him."

"And you are sure he was locked in last night?"

"Positive, Mr Holmes. I did it myself, as I have done every night for several days. I saw him go in and when all was quiet I turned the key. Let me assure you that none of the staff know about this. It is a very informal arrangement that I resorted to quite by chance. You must know that about a month ago Edward announced that he wished to get engaged to a young lady he had met – I don't know where – a foreign person, French, I believe and, not to put too fine a point on it, this lady is not suitable for my son to marry. As I have said, he is now of full age and so I cannot command him as though he were a minor, but he is my son and heir and it is necessary that the lady he chooses as his bride should be a person suitable to follow in the family way and bear his children who will, in turn, succeed him as Lord Challis. I do not know if either of you two gentlemen are fathers, but I am sure you will appreciate my predicament."

"Does Lady Challis have a view point on this?" asked Holmes.

"Well, naturally, she concurs with me."

"What was your son's reaction to this opposition of

yours?" asked Holmes.

"Well at first Edward blustered and said that it was none of our business and so on. Childish nonsense. But after I pointed out to him his obligations and duties, and, not least, that it was not automatic that my wealth would devolve on him if I chose to alter the terms of my will, he began to see sense. I pride myself that I was able to make my son face up to his responsibilities. At present Lady Challis is trying to introduce him to suitable ladies, any of whom would be an ideal wife for him. There are several quite eligible young ladies in London society and I do not wish to impose my will upon him."

"May I ask if these sleepwalking bouts restarted at the time you had this discussion with your son?" I asked.

"What? Well, I don't know. Let me think – no, not at that time. This would be about a month ago, shortly after Christmas, and the sleepwalking has been going on about three weeks. It is only during the last week or so I have taken to locking the door of his room of a night."

"And this morning he escaped from his prison and fled we know not where," said Holmes drily.

"Hardly a prison, Mr Holmes," protested Lord Challis. "In fact he was never aware he was locked in. I did it very discreetly. None of my servants would know. It is a secret between my wife and me. You see his room is next to mine and, as I invariably retire to bed ahead of my son, I am in my room when he comes up. Often he is quite late. Young people seem to prefer to take their enjoyments after midnight. So I am usually in bed, or at least in my room reading, when I see him pass the door and hear him enter his own room. I then wait some minutes until all is quiet and I know he is asleep – he drops off remarkably quickly – I, myself, am a martyr to insomnia. As I say, once he is asleep, I quietly slip out of my room and turn the key in his lock. Then I can sleep easy myself. I am always awake early on a morning but Edward never surfaces before ten o'clock – often not until midday – so as I go downstairs I simply unlock the door and that is that. So you see, it is not so very terrible but I do feel embarrassed as a father having to guard a grown-up son in this manner."

"Your feelings do you credit," said Holmes in a tone of voice in which I alone recognised disapproval.

"I am at my wit's end now, Mr Holmes. This morning there was no Edward anywhere and the door was still locked."

"But it is now late afternoon, why have you delayed in coming to me?"

"Well my staff and I searched the house and garden thoroughly, immediately we discovered that Edward was missing, so that took a little time, then I sent a servant to Scotland Yard to order a detective but there was some delay in that person arriving."

"I know all the inspectors there," said Holmes, "which of them attended upon you?"

"A grumpy little fellow called Lestrade. He refused to do anything. He had a look at the room, said there was no evidence of any crime and that no doubt the missing man would turn up very soon. I remonstrated with the fellow but he was adamant that unless there was a crime he was not obliged to carry out an investigation. He was then brusque to my wife and left leaving her in tears. But surely a grown man being spirited away is a crime. He may have been kidnapped. I find this attitude intolerable from a servant of the public and will raise the matter in the House. That caused the delay to which you refer. I am totally distraught after having spent several hours searching and arguing with the police force. It was this Lestrade fellow who suggested I consulted you. Will you come and investigate, Mr Holmes? I really do not know what to do next."

It was noticeable that a great deal of Lord Challis's initial bluster had disappeared as he revealed himself to be a worried parent who did not know where to turn in his predicament.

"A question or two, if you please, my lord," said Holmes. "Is it not possible that one of your household released your son, if the key was in the lock?"

"That would be quite impossible. The key is not left in the lock. After I have turned the key, locking him in, I place it under my pillow so it is instantly to hand should I need to release him urgently. When I unlock the door in the morning then I leave the key in the lock. No, I am sure no one else would have unlocked the door. In fact, I think I would be certain to hear if anyone came past my door in the night. I am a martyr to insomnia as I have explained. In any case there is no other key to that door. We are not in the habit of locking internal doors at my establishment. The only reason that my son's room has such a lock and key at all, stems from the time some years ago when he previously sleepwalked."

"I cannot really see what I can do, my lord. Presumably you wish your son found," said Holmes.

"Indeed I do. He may be wandering abroad in some kind of stupor, fallen into the Thames, or anything. I beg you to come to my house and investigate."

"I fear there will be little I can do, my lord."

"But surely, man – you can tell how he got out of his locked room and follow clues as to where he has wandered? I was informed that you can follow trails from the slightest clue and you can find evidence that nobody else can see."

"You see, Watson, where your tales have led? I have an unwarranted reputation for second sight," said Holmes sighing.

"Name your price, Mr Holmes, I will pay anything to have my son restored to me."

"I cannot restore your son, Lord Challis. I may be able to find him but I doubt it, as by now your servants will have trampled over your entire premises destroying any clues there were. Also, has it occurred to you that your son may have disappeared quite of his own volition and has no desire to be found? If you wish, I will come to your home and, if it is of use to you, I am sure I can explain how he left the locked room. If I can find indications of the direction in which he has fled I will tell you that too, but I cannot guarantee anything further."

"I will be grateful for anything you can tell me about this sorry affair," said Lord Challis in a far more chastened state than when he arrived.

"Very well. I will return with you. Come, my lord, let us go."

Even as we sped towards Lord Challis's house, the London newspapers were flooding the streets with the sensational story of the escaping nobleman. It is well known that when there is very little news of substance to report, the newspapers fill their pages with contrived taradiddle. In this instance there must have been little of import happening in the country and their blank pages had to be filled somehow – a disappearing heir must have been a godsend to editors. It is a mystery in itself how the newspapers glean information about these private affairs, but it is a rare master that can trust his staff implicitly.

Of course the facts of the case had not at that time been fully established, but there was much play given to the fact that the room in which the heir was locked had only one window which was barred, and only the one door which was impregnable when locked with a varied amount of the locksmith's art according to which journal one read. An enterprising Yankee music hall performer called Harry Houdini trumpeted that he could escape from anything and offered to duplicate the aristocrat's escape. It was the huge publicity surrounding the case of the Hon Edward Dunstable that chiefly enabled that wonderful entertainer to gain the prominence he did in later years.

But as we arrived at Challis House all the furore was unknown to us. We met a very distraught Lady Challis who cried "Thank God, you have come Mr Holmes! We are at our wit's end.  Please find my boy!"

Lord Challis summoned his staff and asked if they had any news to report.  One maid timidly said that she had told my lord that she had thought she had seen Mr Edward leaving the house with his friend Mr Winterton about midnight.

"I have told you, that is impossible, Smith.  I saw him enter his room last night and it was certainly after midnight.  You will only confuse things by repeating such assertions.  Come, gentlemen, I will show you the room."

Lord Challis led us upstairs to a short corridor off the main landing on the first floor.

"As you see, Mr Holmes, there are only the two doors along this corridor.  That one is my room, and the one at the end is Edward's.  We are at the back of the house overlooking the garden where it is quite peaceful.  The front rooms are susceptible to the noise of traffic and I've enough trouble sleeping without the rattling of carriages and clopping of hooves and now these damned motor cars kicking up a din."

"And where is your wife's room?"asked Holmes.

"She has her bedroom and sitting room at the front of the house.  She seems not to be disturbed by noise and the rooms there are larger and loftier."

Holmes took out his glass and examined the key and lock on the outside of the son's door.

"The lock has been recently oiled."

"That is so, Mr Holmes, I did it myself in case Edward should hear the key scrape in the lock."

Holmes examined the area of carpet outside the door and, finally appearing satisfied, he at last opened the door and went in.  The two of us waited outside as he had requested and we heard sundry noises as he obviously crept about the room examining it for clues.

"I note that you have also oiled the hinges of the door, my lord," said Holmes as he finally emerged.

"Why, yes. I thought I may as well while I had the oil

can to hand. I oiled the hinges of my bedroom door too."

"I see," said Holmes. "The window is open; is that how you found it this morning?"

"Oh most certainly. I have touched nothing. But that is not important as Edward invariably sleeps with his window open. He thinks it more healthy, and considering the hours he spends in fetid drinking dens and music halls I am pleased he receives some fresh air somewhere. But as you will have seen, the window is strongly barred; he could not possibly have passed through that way."

"I do not suggest he did. Now may I look at your room, my lord?"

"My room?" cried Lord Challis in astonishment. "What possible use is there in that?"

"I would be obliged if you would humour me. I wish to ascertain where you were and how you could see your son enter his room."

"Very well. Come in." Lord Challis showed us into his room.

"My lord," said Holmes glancing round, "I fail to understand how, from in here, you can see your son enter his room. Please can you explain?"

"Well I cannot, of course, actually see him enter his room. I should explain that this house is entirely lit by the electricity. To illuminate this room I merely have to turn the switch by the door. The corridor outside is lit also, and remains lit throughout the night until it is switched off in the morning, as is all the electricity. Now when I have finished reading and any other preparations for sleep, I turn off that switch at the door and get into the bed which, as you see, faces the door. Do you follow me, Mr Holmes?"

"Perfectly. Pray continue."

"So this room is in darkness, but through the keyhole of the door and a rather ill-fitting jamb I can see light. When my son comes to bed I can tell he is passing the door because the light is momentarily extinguished from my sight by his body. I can also hear his tread, although the corridor is carpeted, and, finally, I can hear his door open and close. So by all these means I can tell when he is in his room. I wait a few minutes then slip out to turn the key and bring it away with me."

"Thank you, you have explained everything very clearly. May I have a look at your charming garden?"

"The garden?" said Lord Challis in amazement. "Of course, but you will not find any sign of Edward there, we have examined it thoroughly."

"I am sure he never went into the garden at all but I would be obliged if you would permit me to enter it," said Holmes blandly.

The garden was not large, perhaps under half an acre, with an enclosing high wall around, the only entrances to it being from the house itself and a large door in the wall that was stoutly barred and padlocked.

"The door is used by the gardeners but it is always barred except when they need to pass through, and I make a point of having it thoroughly checked every night when the house is locked up," said Lord Challis.

"Oh that is very wise. The newspapers tell us that the number of burglaries in London is on the increase. Would you stand just there, my lord, and, Watson there, while I pop back up to your son's room and see you from the window."

"What is this tomfoolery?" snapped Challis.

"Please humour me in this. I do nothing that is not essential," said Holmes and re-entered the house.

As the two of us stood some twenty feet apart, in the spots indicated by Holmes, I endeavoured to assure the noble lord that, eccentric though my friend's actions may seem, they were all very necessary to the conduct of his investigations. It appeared to be a long time before we heard Holmes cry from the window that we may move from our positions, but I spent the interim giving one or two previous examples of Holmes's apparent odd actions and then the reasons therefore, which seemed to mollify Lord Challis.

"Well that seems to be all that I can do for today," said Holmes on returning to us.

"All?  Have you formed no conclusions?" asked the noble lord sadly.

"Indeed I am very clear in my mind about the incidents of last night.  I know what happened as if I had been with you in your room."

"Then, for God's sake, tell me where my son is!" cried Lord Challis. "Assuage his mother's anxiety!"

"Alas, that I cannot do.  I have some further enquiries to make then I will return here tomorrow at six o'clock and reveal all I know.  I trust you will make yourself available?"

"Of course, but my son?  What if he be in some danger?  The delay may be fatal."

"You can rest assured that your son is in no danger.  On the contrary, I think he is probably at this moment happier than he has been for some time.  Until tomorrow evening then."

Just as we were parting, Holmes turned. "How did you find the weather last night, my lord?"

"The weather?  I have no idea.  Does it matter?"

"Indeed, it is most significant.  Good day."

As we returned to Baker Street I was still puzzled by the whole affair but Holmes was whistling cheerily.

"What do you make of this case, Holmes?" I asked, "It seems impossible that a full grown man can escape from his confines without leaving a trace."

"I think you will find the open window is the key to the whole affair, Watson."

"But it is strongly barred, a child could not pass through!" I protested.

"Perfectly true.  I must ask you to excuse me, Watson, I have to pop over to Russell Square."

"Russell Square?"

"There are further enquiries to be made before this affair is tied up." So saying, we parted company and I did not see Holmes again until breakfast the next day.

"Were your enquiries satisfactory, Holmes?" I asked.

"Entirely. I was told what I fully expected to hear. Have you seen the morning paper?"

He threw it across to me and I read a long piece about the mysterious disappearance of the Hon Edward Dunstable. It looked as though the desperate scribe had bolstered his story by interviewing an assortment of fortune tellers, spiritualists and tea cup readers.

"This is sheer twaddle, Holmes!" I cried.

"Of course it is, Watson. But the great British public likes a mystery and if there isn't one then it is necessary to manufacture one for them."

"I take it you have solved the case then?"

"I knew what had happened as soon as the little maid Smith tried to speak out. All my subsequent investigations merely confirmed my thesis. I trust you will come with me on my visit to Lord Challis's house this evening?"

"I would not miss it for the world."

"Good man. I may require you to act as the noble lord's shadow."

Holmes was absent most of the day but he received a delivery from the Lighting Emporium in Oxford Street. What this mysterious item was I had no idea except it was contained in a large square cardboard box and was rather heavy. I was deputed to carry it on our journey to Challis House.

At six o'clock we were back to greet Lord and Lady Challis. He was no longer aggressive but had an air of resignation about him and was as baffled as ever.

"Welcome, Mr Holmes, Dr Watson," said Lady Challis. "I must apologise for my behaviour yesterday when you came but I was greatly upset by Henry's agitation."

"Pray think nothing of it, my lady," I assured her.

"Your distress is perfectly understandable."

"I hope you have an explanation for me, Mr Holmes. I have spent a wretched time since you left. I have not slept a wink," said Lord Challis.

"I cannot tell you where your son is, but I assure you no harm has come to him. I fully expect that you will hear from him within a day or two."

"Do you really think so, Mr Holmes? I have been saying as much, myself, to Henry," said Lady Challis.

"Well that is something I suppose," Lord Challis said grumpily. "But you promised to explain Edward's disappearance."

"I did and I will. I see you have the electricity turned on now, my lord."

"Of course, it is thoroughly dark at four o'clock at this time of year," Lord Challis replied.

Holmes took the parcel I had been carrying and asked permission to visit the bedrooms upstairs. We three were asked to remain where we were until summoned.

"I hope this fellow knows his business," said Lord Challis. "He seems to carry on in a very rum manner."

"Henry, I am sure Mr Holmes is perfectly capable. The Scotland Yard detective recommended him. He said he was the best man you could possibly get," said Lady Challis with a touch of asperity.

I felt that she may sometimes find her husband's brusque manner something of a trial. "You may have every confidence in Holmes," I assured them.

Shortly Holmes returned.

"Now, Lady Challis, I must ask you to remain here while we three go upstairs," said Holmes.

"Oh, dear, am I to miss all the fun?" asked Lady Challis.

"This isn't a game, Dorothy," said Lord Challis reproachfully.

We three men stood in the top corridor as Holmes gave out his instructions. "Now, my lord. I would like to be absolutely clear in my own mind exactly what were the movements of you and your son on the night. If I could trouble you to re-enact your activities of two nights ago, Dr Watson here will act as your shadow, while I will play the part of your son."

"Very well, whatever you think is necessary. I should have thought it was all perfectly clear."

"I'm sure it is, my lord, but you will have heard that my investigations are most thorough. Presumably, the very first thing you did was switch on the light?"

"No, that was already lit. My valet had prepared the room. He always leaves me with brandy and soda and a biscuit on a tray, on my bedside table. I usually read a chapter of a book sitting in my chair. I then turn off the light switch and cross to the bed and climb in."

"And two nights ago you did all this?" asked Homes.

"Yes, yes!" said Lord Challis testily. "I invariably perform the same ritual every night. Is all this really relevant?"

"Now I want you and Watson to enter your room, close the door, turn out your light and wait for the space of three minutes. Watch and listen carefully. Is that clear? It will not be necessary to get into bed. "

"Perfectly clear."

"Then when you have heard me, as your son, enter my room please wait three further minutes then you may emerge and lock my door just as you did at the time. Having done that please return to your room and wait. Do you understand?"

"Perfectly."

Lord Challis and I entered his room and carried out Holmes's directions. I could plainly see the light from the corridor through the keyhole and the ill-fitting door. All was silent then we heard Holmes outside walking noisily along the corridor. Holmes can move as soundlessly as a wraith when he chooses so I realized he was deliberately making a noise in order that we could follow his movements and sure enough we saw the light momentarily blocked by his body as he passed our door.

"You see, Doctor, there he goes, and listen, there is the sound of his door closing."

"Exactly as it did on the night."

"Exactly."

"And the time was?"

"Oh I'm not precisely sure. I could not see my clock as the room was in darkness of course. It would be about midnight, I suppose, because I remember thinking that, for once, Edward was not very long after me coming to bed. Usually there is quite a lapse of time."

"Right, let us go and lock Mr Holmes in his bedroom," I said. We emerged from our room and in a couple of paces reached the door of the other bedroom which Lord Challis locked. "So, my lord, we have duplicated exactly all the movements of the night in question just as Holmes requested."

"That is true. Although I fail to see what all this proves."

"I confess neither do I, but Mr Holmes does nothing without a purpose. Rest assured there is a reason for all this. Come we must return to your room." While we waited I gazed round Lord Challis's bedroom. It was austere, like the man himself, with a minimum of luxury, an easy chair being the only source of comfort apart from the large bed. There was a tap at the door. We opened it to find Lady Challis outside.

"Henry, you are to pretend the night has now passed and it is morning. Mr Holmes has instructed that you unlock and open Edward's door," she said, standing to one side to allow us to pass her in order to carry out that action.

Lord Challis unlocked the door and threw it open. "No one is here!" he cried. I pushed past him into the room and was astounded to see a whirling electric fan standing in the middle of the floor and no sign of Holmes anywhere.

"Is this some sort of joke, Doctor?" cried Lord Challis in anger.

"Not at all, my lord, I have gone to some lengths to prove to you how your son disappeared." We turned to see Holmes leaning nonchalantly against the wall behind us all.

"I don't understand this, Mr Holmes. Are you saying my son was never in his room at all?" asked Lady Challis.

"Precisely. Lord Challis made one fundamental mistake in telling himself the sequence of events and, on the basis of that error, has built up the events to an impossible conclusion. As soon as he told me that it was impossible to leave the room by the window or any other way than via the door, then logic told me your son had left by that door. My examination here confirmed that. So if he left by the door, he could not have been locked in as you, my lord, thought. When you then disclosed the process of how you assumed he entered the room, I knew that was the flaw. In your description to me at our rooms in Baker Street, you said you saw him enter his room. Until I examined the premises here I did not realise this was completely untrue. You could not see him at all, but your ears heard the familiar noises of steps and doors opening and closing. Your brain put two and two together and made five."

"You accuse me of jumping to conclusions?"

"It is impossible to tell which way a person is moving when looking through a keyhole or slot. Your son's body, blocking the light of the corridor, could have been moving equally to the left or to the right. The effect would have been exactly the same – a brief momentary blockage of the light. You thought he was going towards his room when in reality he was going away from it."

"But the door. I heard the door closing after his shadow had passed. That means he must have used the door after passing my room," said Lord Challis.

"Normally I would have agreed with you, my lord, but, should there be a delay in the door closing, then it would be possible for such an occurrence to be misinterpreted."

"But how could the door close by its own volition if Edward had already passed by?" interjected Lady Challis.

"You will recall that I enquired about the weather in the night. In Baker Street there was considerable wind. I found by enquiry it was the same in this part of London. Your son left the door of his room open, probably fearing that you, as a light sleeper, might hear it click if he closed it. Immediately his plan was thwarted by a gust of wind from the window blowing the door closed. Your son had much on his mind and it did not occur to him to close his window. As soon as the door blew closed, aided I must say by the recent oiling of the hinges by your good self, Mr Dunstable fled in great haste before you were roused to prevent his exit. You were roused, but instead of going in pursuit, you assumed he had gone in the other direction and entered his room rather than leaving it. You thus locked the door on an empty room."

"Well, Mr Holmes, I think you have made a fool of me."

"No, my lord, I have solved the problem of your son vanishing from a locked room, that is all. I have no idea where he is. I have no suggestions on how to find him. I can assure you he left under no duress and I think if you will examine your maid Smith more thoroughly, you will find he left in the company of one of his chums. If you enquire at the temporary residence of his French friend in Russell Square you will find she, too, has mysteriously disappeared. Our agreement was to explain your son's disappearance which I am sure I have done to your satisfaction, my lord."

"Mr Holmes, I am puzzled still by one thing," said Lady Challis. "You say the wind blew the door closed on that night?"

"That is correct."

"But there is no wind at the present time, yet still the door blew shut."

"Ah, yes. I am afraid the absence of wind would have rendered my ocular demonstration incomplete so I was obliged to simulate the effect of the wind by the use of one of the excellent electric fans manufactured by the General Electric Company of America. When I visited you yesterday I observed that not only did you have the electric lights but you also had a facility for attaching other electrical apparatus to your circuit. Please accept the fan as a gift, it will be invaluable when the humid summer weather arrives."

"You have solved the problem with great skill, Mr Holmes. I pray you are also correct about our hearing from our son shortly."

On the way back to 221B Baker Street, I ventured to say that one aspect of the investigation still puzzled me.

"Why did you place Lord Challis and myself on the lawn while you took a sighting from the window? In fact why were we in the garden at all?"

Holmes laughed. "My purpose in going into the garden was to ascertain if the trees had been damaged by wind. Although the noble lord was unaware of the fact, the wind had been strong that night as the many twigs scattered about the garden readily proved. But the other, I confess, was merely a ruse to keep the noble lord away from me sufficiently long enough to speak to Smith, the little maid who actually saw Mr Dunstable depart the house with his friend Mr Nigel Winterton."

"Well I assured Lord Challis that you never did anything without a good reason."

"Should you ever write-up this case for one of your sensational features, Watson, what conclusions would you draw from it?"

"Well, not to believe everything an eye witness says. He may be in error."

"Yes. We have a tendency to believe what a man says because he is one of the great and powerful. The little maid was hushed up because, although she knew the truth, it did not fit in with what her superior wanted to believe. It may be that, when our nation educates its masses as well as its privileged, a time will come when we disbelieve everything our masters tell us."

As the world now knows, Edward Dunstable reappeared some four days later with a new wife. He had been married in Paris, the best man being the groom's friend Mr Winterton.

\* \* \*

Although I had shared rooms with my friend Mr Sherlock Holmes for several years there were many things that I did not know about him. I was never certain of his exact age, for instance, and I was unable to celebrate his birthday since that, as with so many other things, was a date he kept secret. Holmes was not as other men and the year passed without his remarking in any way such milestones as Easter, birthdays, Trafalgar Day and so on.

But even Holmes could not pretend that Christmas did not exist and latterly he had even permitted Mrs Hudson to sprinkle our rooms with the traditional holly and mistletoe, although he had forbidden that good soul to provide a decorated tree as is now the tradition.

As Christmas 1905 approached I was thrown into my usual dilemma of what to buy Holmes for a Christmas gift. He did not lay much store on worldly goods and we had long since come to an accommodation whereby we bought each other a mere token of the festive season. I could normally expect Holmes to give me a book and I must say that over the years he has provided me with some excellent reads, although the year he bought me a work on comparative religions gave me deeply furrowed brows well into mid-summer. For my part I found my friend a very difficult man for whom to find a suitable present. In desperation I usually ended up buying him an inordinate amount of his favourite shag.

This year I promised myself that I would start thinking about Holmes's present very early and would come up with some stunning and clever idea. But alas, here we were at the 22nd December and I was still as brainless as in November. Holmes was out, I knew not where, but he never confided his multifarious comings and goings to me unless he wanted my company. As it was a bitterly cold day I had not ventured out and was enjoying crouching by the fire in the hastening gloom reading the festive edition of our local weekly newspaper.

I was musing to myself how the contents of a local newspaper that served a specific town or district, whilst fascinating to the inhabitants of that place, was of total disinterest to anybody who lives elsewhere.

Notices about church services, talks in obscure halls about dull subjects, meetings of this society and that club, amateur entertainments and sporting fixtures – what a gallimaufry of things to do amongst the gracious squares, wide boulevards, mean streets and lowly dwellings. Then it caught my eye: an announcement advertising the new season of the Baker Street Chamber Music Society. The name was not totally unfamiliar as I had occasionally seen modest posters proclaiming events held by this organisation but I had not really taken cognisance of them. The advertisement stated that new members were always welcome and the annual subscription was very modest. Here was the answer to my problem! I would buy Holmes a subscription to this society. He was a music lover and often went to concerts. Here was a programme on his very doorstep – one each month during the winter season. The society met at the Grafton Galleries in Bond Street which was but a stone's throw from 221b. I made a note of the secretary's address and determined to sally forth in the morning to buy a subscription.

The following day I descended to find Holmes at breakfast and in a whimsical mood.

"Just in time, Watson, if you had delayed any longer all Mrs Hudson's excellent crumpets would have completely vanished."

"You are in a good temper, Holmes," said I as I lifted up the lid of the warming dish, "are you anticipating the jolly season of merriment and goodwill to all men?"

"Not so, Watson. There is no better opportunity for crime to flourish than in this happy and smiling season of goodwill. Theft is never easier than when the booty may be concealed in capacious handbags or beneath flowing cloaks in crowded streets and the scream, the drunkard's blow, are so readily drowned by caroling young voices singing 'God rest ye merry, gentlemen!'"

"You always see the worst side of mankind, Holmes," said I, sadly.

"And why not, when my profession reveals it to me constantly. However, tonight I am taking myself off to hear the sublime artistry of Kreisler."

"Who's he, one of your fiddlers?" I asked in what I intended to be a jovial manner but which came out rather grumpily.

"The depths of your ignorance constantly amazes me, Watson. Kreisler has been lauded as the most exciting soloist of the age. I am surprised that even you should not know his name considering how often it has been in the public press of late and that you spend a good deal of your day ploughing through morning and evening papers."

"You know Gilbert and Sullivan's stuff is more in my line, Holmes."

"You are guilty of living in the past, Watson. Sullivan has been dead these five years. We are now in the 20th century. Victoria is no more."

"God rest her soul."

"Keep up with the times, old fellow. Did you not see that the American Wright brothers have flown their flying machine in the air for a distance of 24 miles over a space of almost forty minutes?"

"I did. Nothing more than an elaborate kite with a motor attached."

"You are grumpy this morning; has something upset you?" asked Holmes.

"No, no," I sighed, "only this wretched infernally cold weather."

"I rather think something infernal should be hot," chuckled Holmes.

"All I know is that my time in Afghanistan has made my constitution better able to withstand heat rather than cold."

"Well I think this morning I will prepare myself for this evening by having a shot at playing one the pieces Kreisler is to perform tonight."

"Oh, if you are going to do that then I prefer to brave the elements."

"Just teasing you, old fellow. I shall do no such thing but I will peruse the score."

"I have to go out anyway, I have business to attend to."

The conversation then petered out as I tucked into my breakfast with gusto and Holmes pottered off to his room. As I ate I metaphorically hugged myself with the thought of what a perfect gift I had planned for my friend. The address of the secretary of the Baker Street Chamber Music Society was given in the advertisement but I did not think it wise to rely on the post at this particularly busy time of year so determined, as the street mentioned was nearby, to go round clutching my guineas to obtain a season ticket in person.

Outside I found not only was the weather exceptionally cold but a blustery wind had sprung up and as I passed the ends of side streets the wind whipping down nearly knocked me off my feet. It was the sort of day when I would cheerfully have remained indoors throughout, viewing the world through the pages of the public press.

On arriving at the secretary's address the door was opened by that personage himself – a fellow of indeterminate age but quite likely old enough to be my father. I explained my mission and was invited in.

"I do not normally have callers at my door. People usually order their subscriptions by post. It is most irregular," said the ancient.

"I thought it unwise to trust the post, being Christmas shortly. I understand some deliveries are not getting through until the following day. As I live nearby it seemed a sensible thing to do. I trust this does not offend you?"

" Oh no, not at all, my dear sir. Not at all. It is irregular most certainly, but not offensive. Oh no, by no means offensive. As you say, quite sensible. Indeed most sensible. In fact it is most helpful. It saves my having to deal with cheques and enclosures, posting out receipts and so on. But, you know, you could have enrolled in person at any of our meetings. A lot of our members do that. They join at the first meeting. Perhaps that was not clear from the advertisement?"

I assured the garrulous old fellow that I had understood that but, as I wished to buy the subscription as a surprise gift for someone else, that was hardly possible. He seemed to think the idea an extraordinary one.

"Oh, so this subscription is not for your good self? A present for another person. Well that is exceedingly beneficent of you. Exceedingly so. Are you, perhaps, already one of our members? I don't recognise you, I must say. But we have so many members now – in excess of 300 but, of course, not all come to every concert. We usually get about 200 which is fortunate because the hall can seat barely more. We meet at the Grafton Galleries in Bond Street. It is totally full occasionally but it generally averages at 200. If all the members attended every single concert then we would have to seek a larger hall. Alternatively we could have a repeat performance of each concert.

Engage the performers for two nights rather than one. But of course that would put the costs up – double fees and accommodation. Musicians are so expensive these days. We try to keep our subscription down to a reasonable level. We have found that our more – how shall I say this? Our more prosperous members often include a voluntary addition to their subscription. It is quite spontaneous and most good of them but it does mean that we can offer a discount for our lower class members. There are many working people who appreciate good music and we do not want to discourage them. I know personally of several working men – and their wives too – who delight in coming to our soirées. Yes. Yes. Indeed."

During this long and muttered monologue I interjected at first with "Really" and "Indeed" and so on but when it was clear he had virtually forgotten my very presence I ceased the attempt to be polite. The ramblings were accompanied by his opening sundry drawers in a cabinet and grubbing about amongst papers, occasionally pausing while he peered in bafflement at a certain text before carrying on. Finally having assembled the necessary items he needed to attend to my request, he turned and addressed me directly.

"Of course our season runs from September to April. Eight concerts on the last Wednesday of the month. So the season is now at the mid point."

"I understood from your advertisement that I could take out a subscription for the remaining half of the season at half the full rate," I said.

"Assuredly, assuredly. The full subscription is five guineas for eight concerts so it will be exactly half that amount for the remaining four." I nodded my assent. "Now, sir, may I ask your name?"

"Dr John Watson."

"Ah, a medical man. Not the first one in our membership by any means, oh no. We have several physicians in our fold."

"I am not to be the new member," I said.

"Oh, I thought you had come to take out a subscription to our society?" he replied with a puzzled gaze.

"I do wish to take out a subscription, but on behalf of somebody else. My friend Mr Sherlock Holmes."

"Ah I see. So I am not to put your name on the form but that of your friend."

"Exactly."

"And what is your friend's name?" asked he peering over his spectacles.

"Mr Sherlock Holmes," I repeated with as much grace as I could muster.

"And Mr Holmes's address?"

"221b Baker Street"

"Oh that is very convenient. That is quite near where we hold our recitals."

"Quite. That's why I thought the subscription would be an ideal Christmas present. Mr Holmes is an ardent music lover," I explained, raising my voice and speaking as though to a partially deaf person.

"Oh a Christmas present. What a good idea. What number did you say in Baker Street?"

"221b."

"There we are. I've written the name and the address on the form, perhaps you would be so good as to sign it then I will make out your membership card."

I signed the form and handed it back. I was beginning to think it would have been quicker to apply by post. It would certainly have been simpler.

"Oh but this signature does not say Sherlock Holmes!" cried the secretary.

"No," I patiently explained, "that is my signature, John Watson MD. I am paying you for the subscription on behalf of my friend Mr Sherlock Holmes whose details I have just furnished."

"Ah. Perhaps I should put your name on the card?" he mused.

"No, I hardly think so. It is Mr Holmes who will attend the concerts. He would not wish to masquerade as Dr Watson."

"No, no, I do see that." The secretary paused as if in the grip of some brain numbing problem. "I have it. Perhaps you would be so good as to append under your signature *per pro* Mr Sherlock Holmes."

He handed the paper back to me and I did as he bade. During the next five minutes he produced a bunch of cards approximately the size of a common post card bound with an elastic band; removed one, folded it in half; and, with a steel pen, laboriously wrote on a printed dotted line the name Mr Sherlock Holmes. The only wonder was that he did not use a quill pen and sprinkle powder on the ink. Having handed over the money and gained possession of this vital card I hastened to make my leave. It was difficult to do this with good grace as the old man still rambled on.

"I'm sure your friend will enjoy the rest of the season. We have some very special performers coming. The Prague Quartet is due in April. They are from Prague you know. They are world renowned exponents of Dvorjak. We are very fortunate to get them. They are touring this country throughout April. Very expensive. We are having to compensate by presenting a very economical March concert. Students from the Royal College of Music. Very talented of course, but not really professional. We pride ourselves on not using amateur performers no matter how talented. But the highlight of the entire year is our very next meeting. In January we are to have Signor Guido Salvato the Gloved Pianist."

As he paused, after announcing this with something of a flourish, I took the opportunity to break in and say "Thank you so much. I must be off as I have an urgent appointment. I have a patient who is in middle of a heart attack and needs my immediate ministrations. I'm sure you understand. Goodbye."

I grabbed my hat which had reposed on a chair throughout my visit and bolted for the door leaving the old fellow muttering "A heart attack, good gracious me, how awful."

\* \* \*

On Christmas morning Holmes and I had an unspoken pact that we would always breakfast together. Usually each breakfasted as we arose, neither man waiting for the other and Holmes often remained in his dressing gown or appeared not at all. But on this special day he made a point of appearing dressed and ready for the day, waiting for me should I be after him. Our habit of perusing the morning papers while we ate being also suspended on this occasion.

Holmes, not a man to wallow in sentiment, made a special effort to be agreeable as he knew it was on days like these that I especially missed my late wife and the blessings of family life. We chatted pleasantly of this and that and recalled previous adventures together, naturally centering around the case of the Blue Carbuncle that occupied us during the Christmas of 1889. On finishing our meal we exchanged our modest gifts. Holmes had bought me a book called *The Club of Queer Trades* by Chesterton which I looked forward to reading. As Holmes never read fiction I can only imagine that the title had caught his imagination. I watched eagerly to see his reaction as he opened my gift. As it was nothing more substantial than a card in an envelope he was no doubt using all his powers of deduction to discern what on earth it could be.

"Thank you, Watson. Most kind," he said as he gazed at the card with a total lack of enthusiasm.

"The Baker Street Chamber Music Society holds its recitals at the Grafton Galleries in Bond Street so it is exceedingly convenient. And they have a programme of top-class musicians engaged. I spoke to the secretary himself."

"Indeed."

"Members may take guests for a modest extra charge so I could accompany you on occasion."

"No doubt. Well I think Mrs Hudson has set us up for the day. I shall be lunching with brother Mycroft at the Diogenes Club of course. Will you be going to your cousin as usual?"

"Yes, but I will be back for dinner. Mrs Hudson has promised us salmon and a goose plus her excellent plum pudding," I replied.

Holmes always took luncheon with his brother on Christmas Day; it was about the only occasion when the two brothers behaved like normal people. I, myself, was guilty of a lie. I had no cousin to go to, in fact I could acknowledge fewer relatives than Homes. Two or three years ago when Holmes was off to meet his brother he suddenly raised the question as to how I should occupy the festive day, a thought that had never troubled him previously. As I did not wish to embarrass him by forcing him to include me in the family lunch, on the spur of the moment I invented a cousin with a large family who lived at South Norwood who always insisted I spent the day with them. Each year this lie had developed and I had come to regard Cousin Simon and his wife Susan with their brood of little ones as though they truly existed.

In actual fact I spent my day assisting at St Bartholomew's Hospital where I helped to deputise for married doctors who valued a few hours at home with their families. It was a voluntary initiative that I first took to for purely selfish reasons after the death of my wife. I did not want to sit alone at home brooding on my dear departed love and had continued the practice thereafter, long after time had eased the pain. Holmes and I agreed to meet at our rooms to dine at eight.

"This is not a happy start to the new year, Watson. Three weeks into 1906 and not a vestige of a case," complained Holmes.

"Perhaps the criminal fraternity of London have taken a new year resolution to mend their ways," I said jocularly.

"But my brain will atrophy without something to stimulate it. Ennui is my curse. You know I hate being idle."

"I thought you were in the middle of some scientific experiment."

"A mere diversion, Watson. A poor substitute for action."

As January 23rd – the date of the first concert – approached, Holmes had made no mention of my gift since receiving it in an offhand manner on Christmas morning. I suspected he had no intention of attending the first concert of his subscription. Indeed I fear he did not appreciate my carefully thought out gift at all and that I had wasted my money. It was probably a mistake on my part as on many occasions in the past when I had pointed out advertisements for concerts he had made it clear that he did not wish to listen to anyone but the finest talents and that his musical interests resided entirely in the violin. I well recall his saying "When you have been transported to the heavens by the sublime artistry of Sarasate, Joachim, Naruda, to have to suffer the pitiful scrapings of professional hacks is tedious in the extreme." Holmes can be very hurtful at times and tact has never been one of his strengths. I determined to broach the subject in defiance of his apparent apathy.

"This concert on Thursday sounds particularly intriguing," I said.

"What concert is that, Watson?" he replied as he crouched over his test tubes.

"Signor Guido Salvato the Gloved Pianist from Italy," I said. "The first concert you may attend with the present I bought you."

There was a long silence as he continued his work then he turned round to face me. "Oh Watson, I am unable to attend on Thursday. I have a previous engagement. Perhaps you can go in my place."

"I thought you were languishing with boredom as you had no cases?" I said.

"True, Watson, true. It is unfortunate that the concert is on the very day I have an important meeting. Any other day and I would have welcomed the diversion."

"So you are unable to go on Thursday?"

"Alas, no."

"And you cannot change your appointment to another night?"

"Regrettably, no."

"It's a pity the concert is not on Wednesday, then. You would have been free that night," said I with a sigh.

"Yes, a great pity. But there we are." He turned to attend to his experiment. I took out my diary and made a great play of looking up the date.

"Well, how exceedingly fortunate. I mistook the date. The concert is after all on Wednesday!" I cried.

There was a long silence as I looked at the back of my friend. He threw up his hands and laughed out loud. "It's a fair cop, guv! You've done me bang to rights!" he said mockingly in a broad Cockney accent. "Watson, you are a devious man. You present this open and honest facade to the world but inside you are full of cunning and intrigue."

"It's only a musical evening, Holmes, you will probably enjoy it."

"Very well, I agree to attend on one condition."

"And what's that."

"That you shall suffer with me.

* * *

~ 32 ~

As we made our way on foot down Baker Street towards the venue I remarked on the increasing number of motor cars that were appearing on the roads.

"Modern times, Watson. It seems no time ago that the authorities were forecasting that London would be submerged in horse dung to a depth of three feet and drastic action would be necessary."

"I wonder what this Gloved Pianist will be like?"

"Almost sure to be awful, Watson. He sounds more like a music hall performer than a serious musician. It is a mere stunt to wear gloves to play a keyboard."

"Actually, Holmes, they do say that his hands have been blemished by some disease or disfigurement and that is why he had to resort to wearing gloves. He had a career as a serious pianist before having recourse to them."

"I should imagine his career as a serious pianist was going nowhere so he has resorted to this ploy to give himself a boost."

"You are a cynic, Holmes."

"Very likely," he replied cryptically.

At the door were two sturdy fellows who saw to our wants and passed us into the hall. At a table I noticed the ancient secretary and counted my blessings that Holmes did not have to deal with him. The salon where the concert was to take place was the largest gallery, a lofty elegant room with rows of chairs facing a low platform decorated with potted palms and music stands. On the walls were some very peculiar pictures. Most seemed to be mere repetitious patterns in bright colours. Twisted flowers and foliage seemed particularly popular. We were handed programmes on taking our seats which were somewhat to the rear, a goodly audience being already in place ready for the evening's attractions. We were to have a varied programme with some Boccherini by a string quartet and a couple of folk songs by Walter Porter, who was also the chairman for the proceedings, before the star attraction appeared.

"It is quite a respectable gathering, Holmes. That chap there taking a great interest in the piano is Edmund Redvers-Gordon the famous explorer. I thought he had left on an expedition. It said in the papers he was off to Africa again."

"Oh, Watson, the faith you have in the contents of newspapers," chided Holmes.

~ ~ ~ Edmund Redvers-Gordon was a scion of a family that could trace it's ancestry back to the times of Richard Coeur d'Lion. Effigies of Redvers knights of old could be found in Ely Cathedral and Tewkesbury Abbey. By the 19th century the Redvers-Gordons no longer had claim to nobility and aristocracy although immediate ancestors included a major who served with distinction at Waterloo, two bishops, and a surgeon who pioneered a new technique in the field of urology. But they were still sufficiently rich and Edmund's father bought an estate called Shrivers which contained a manor house dating back to the 15th century, a farm, several cottages and thousands of acres of land. Redvers-Gordon senior immediately demolished the ancient manor house and built a modern expansive villa in classical style. It was in this house that Edmund was born.

Edmund Redvers-Gordon was the third son in a family of eight children and was a boy of questing curiosity. He was tutored at home by a succession of men who had to be better and better qualified as the boy grew and his mind developed. His thirst for knowledge was insatiable and his brain was like a sponge that absorbed all manner of facts. It was this trait, persisting throughout his adulthood, that enabled him to produce the most esoteric facts over a wide range of subjects in a conversation on practically any matter.

He was fond of exploring the family's extensive grounds which had been landscaped into hillocks and valleys, copses and lakes and extensive flower beds containing plants from all over the world. As he grew,

Edmund would wander further afield and was often absent at lunch time, turning up tired and dishevelled at the end of the afternoon. Once, when he was eight years old, he was still missing at dinner time and his anxious parents sent out a search party but he could not be found. He was away all night and the local police were alerted. He rolled up next morning shortly after breakfast to say he had walked to Peascod Forest, some fifteen miles away, and darkness had fallen before he could get all the way back. He had spent the night in a providential hayrick and continued his journey at sunrise. When asked why he should wish to go to Peascod Forest he simply replied that he wanted to see what it was like.

Although Mrs Redvers-Gordon was reluctant to part with her son, who was her youngest boy and something of a favourite, her husband was insistent that he needed the discipline of school and thus Edmund was packed off to a prep school before going on the traditional route of Eton, where he was a great asset to the first XI and his bowling exploits still talked of many years later, thence to Cambridge where he was a renowned sportsman awarded Blues in rowing, rugby and athletics. But always his main interest was to see the world. He wanted to go to places just to see what they were like. To his parents' displeasure he enrolled with the Bechuanaland Field Force under Sir Charles Warren during the Warren Expedition in Bechuanaland in 1884 but he soon realised that he did not want to be involved in politics, trade or exploitation in these African territories that were being scrambled over by the great powers in Europe. Thus he resigned and took himself to South America where, forming his own expedition, he explored the Amazon jungle. He spent four years investigating the many tributaries of the mighty Amazon river including the Purus, Ucayali and Xingu, and found various indigenous tribes that had never seen a white man. During this time he based himself at Manaus and relied on money transfers from an indulgent father.

On his return to England he spent several weeks closeted in his room, emerging only to take meals as he poured his experiences into a lengthy book that would not only reveal his many discoveries but, he hoped, help fund his future explorations. He barely had time to open all the packing cases and see once more all the many artefacts, seeds and samples he had dispatched to himself over the years.

In 1888 the extension of the Trans-Caspian railway enabled Redvers-Gordon to fulfil a childhood ambition when he visited the fabled city of Samarkand. One of the oldest cities in the world, an important stop on the ancient Silk Route from China, the romantic legends of this city had been greatly responsible for firing the imagination of the little lad. However, whereas twenty years earlier it had been under the rule of the Muslim Emir of Bukhara it was now the capital of Russian Turkestan having been taken by force by the Russian Colonel Alexander Abramov who largely rebuilt the place. Although not the fabled city of the *Arabian Nights* it did not disappoint Redvers-Gordon nor quench his venturous spirit.

He now departed to Borneo inspired by a chance meeting with Sir Charles Brooke the White Rajah of Sarawak. He explored the depths of the jungle but was repelled by the dominance of Brooke over the Iban and Dyak tribes. Redvers-Gordon's quest was always to see the world as it was, not to alter it by bringing western ideas of civilisation, although he was perforce obliged to acknowledge the presence of traders and missionaries was often greatly enabling to his expeditions. The main benefit from this brief sojourn in Borneo was gaining the friendship and, later, finance from Baroness Angela Burdett-Coutts who was a close friend of Rajah Brooke; she was a generous philanthropist and a great believer in the development of Africa.

Edmund Redvers-Gordon suffered from the death of his father who left all his property to his eldest son Ralph.

Edmund and Ralph had never been close and the brother was reluctant to fund Edmund's expeditions. As a result Edmund returned to Africa where he made a point of seeking out areas as yet untouched by the hand of the white man. He went on expeditions to Nyasaland, Matebeleland and Somaliland, but found these becoming places of colonial development and went on to the more remote inhospitable areas of Congo, Sokoto – where he was one of the few Europeans to reach the fabled city of Timbuktu – and Bornu. Each time after returning home he wrote of his travels. Home was now a large house in Hampstead which his brother had provided for him on the basis that he should no longer look to him for subsidy. This house, stocked with artefacts from his travels, was his refuge but he was only really at home in the jungles or desert plains of Africa.

Edmund Redvers-Gordon had grown into a man well over six feet in height, craggy of visage and weather-beaten by the tropical sun. He was of good health and strength in spite of succumbing to insidious tropical diseases that held up the progress of his wanderings. In the Congo he had suffered for  three months from abscesses deforming his leg with inflammation, causing intense pain, which was only relieved temporarily by deep incisions permitting copious discharge; his strength was prostrated and walking impossible. Many cures were attempted by the natives, including a poultice made of cow-dung, salt, and mud from the lake, placed on hot. Whether these were responsible for ending the disease or whether it ran its natural course cannot be known, but diseases and ju-ju cures were no detriment to this intrepid man who, even at the age of 45, still wanted to go to places just to see what they were like.  ~ ~ ~

"Well you know those two, Holmes." I nodded to a distinguished couple near the front at the side. "Lord and Lady Challis.  You recall how you explained their son's midnight disappearance. We ought to go over and say hello. I wonder if there is an interval when we may do so?"

"It appears that Lady Challis has been unwell recently," said Holmes.

"Has she? Where did you learn that?"

"There is a walking stick under her chair."

"It could be her husband's."

"I think not, Watson. Lord Challis would undoubtedly have a much stronger, more masculine, stick. It is definitely a lady's."

"Well she is still a handsome woman but she may be feeling her age."

"Possibly, but she does not appear at all enfeebled in any way. I think the stick not habitual as she spent a minute or two at a loss as to where to put it. She tried hooking it over the chair in front, then stood to hook it over her own chair before finally placing it on the floor underneath. If she is a long-standing member here, one would assume she had long since decided how to cope with her stick if it were a regular appendage. I think you will find she has had an accident or disease quite recently that has affected her walking."

"How do you know they are regulars, Holmes. They may be newcomers like us."

"The front of the programme states 'founded in 1888 by Lord and Lady Challis'. Inside it states 'President Lord Challis'. I think we can assume the noble lord and his lady are habitués."

"We should say hello. The concert's not due to start just yet. I'll pop over and pay our respects," I said.

"Do as you wish, Watson," sighed Holmes with an air of insufferable boredom.

So I went over and greeted the noble lord "Perhaps you don't remember me, Lord Challis? Dr John Watson, I attended your house when your son went missing."

"Of course, with Mr Sherlock Holmes. How do you

do?" he politely replied, shaking my hand. He turned to his wife. "You remember Dr Watson and Mr Holmes, don't you, my dear?"

"Of course, how are you Doctor? Are you a member of our little clan?" said Lady Challis.

"No, no. I am with Mr Holmes. He is a member; I am here as his guest."

"Mr Holmes a member? I didn't know that," said Lord Challis in surprise.

"He has only just joined, this is his first visit," I explained.

"Well I'm sure he will enjoy himself, Dr Watson," Lady Challis said, "we have such congenial evenings here at the Society." I murmured some pleasantry and was just about to leave them when a dandified young fellow thrust himself into our conversation.

"Good evening, Lady Challis, I trust your leg is healing satisfactorily," said the newcomer politely.

"Slowly, Aubrey, but it is a great nuisance, I must confess. I must be more circumspect when alighting from my husband's motor car."

"Good evening, Morello," said Lord Challis in a civil but somewhat frigid manner before Lady Challis continued "Oh Dr Watson this is one of our most talented musicians Mr Aubrey Morello. Dr Watson is a colleague of the famous detective Sherlock Holmes."

"Indeed? Pleased to meet you, sir," said Aubrey Morello shaking my hand affably.

"Are you to play for us this evening?" I asked.

"No, not tonight. I have played several concerts for the Society, but tonight the honours go to an Italian gentleman who claims to be a pianist," replied Morello with a smirk.

"Come, come, Aubrey," twinkled Lady Challis, "you cannot play all the recitals. You must allow someone else the opportunity."

Morello gave an audible snort, bowed, said "Excuse

me," turned and left us.

"Insolent puppy," muttered Lord Challis.

I suspected there was more to this rather odd little exchange than I could understand. Although it had nothing to do with me, Lady Challis must have felt that some explanation was necessary and she said "Mr Morello has the artistic temperament. He is a dear boy but does tend to have violent dislikes. Though he is very talented and we always engage him to play when we have soirées at Challis House and many of our friends have taken him up too."

~ ~ ~ Aubrey Morrell was an infant prodigy. Both his parents were musicians, his mother was a well respected piano teacher in the spa town of Cheltenham and his father, who also played the piano as well as several brass instruments, was a mainstay of the Cheltenham Theatre Royal resident pit orchestra. The tiny Aubrey was not a biddable child and prone to temper tantrums from an early age. His mother found that the most satisfactory way to deal with these disobedient bouts was to sit her son under the grand piano whilst she gave lessons to her many pupils. This seemed to have a soothing effect on the infant and he would sit silently for many hours in this position.

One day his mother, being occupied elsewhere in the house, became aware of the sound of someone tinkling on her piano and in a fluster, thinking it was a pupil who had arrived unexpectedly, rushed down to see the six year old Aubrey standing at the piano playing in a creditable fashion on the keyboard. Mrs Morrell immediately placed her son on the stool and over the next few weeks gave him every encouragement and assistance. He was soon playing to a high standard and reading music. From that moment there was no holding this prodigious child back as he mastered piece after piece. Mr Morrell became convinced his son was a second Mozart especially when, at the age of ten, he started composing piano solos.

When he gained 12 years old there was no doubt the young Aubrey Morrell was a peculiarly talented boy and his father, via his contacts at the theatre, arranged for his son to give a public recital there. This event was greeted with great acclaim and on the strength of the reception Mr Morrell gave up his job in the pit orchestra and arranged a nationwide tour for his son. Acting as chaperone and manager Mr Morrell took his son to the spa towns of Harrogate, Leamington, Bath, Scarborough and Tunbridge Wells where he gave solo recitals for the pleasure of the visitors taking the waters. He was acclaimed in all these places so Mr Morrell then arranged a second tour along the south coastal resorts. By this means the boy earned quite a large amount of money for one so young.

Further concerts followed over the next two years but Aubrey was disinclined to travel and much of this period was spent in begrudging acquiescence to his father's wishes. At the age of 14 Aubrey auditioned for the professors of the Royal College of Music which had been founded under the auspices of the Prince of Wales six years previously. He so impressed them that he was admitted as the youngest pupil to attend up to that time. Public performing by students was frowned upon so Aubrey was not heard much at this period. At the age of 16 Aubrey went to the Paris Conservatoire, one of the very few English musicians to do so. Of a naturally sullen disposition Aubrey was not happy there as his fellow students, as well as his tutors, were chiefly of French or Italian nationality. His particular *bête noir* was a student from Palermo in Sicily by the name of Salvato who aroused great animosity in the rapidly maturing Morrell. Whether this was because of musical differences or concerning some amorous matter is not known.

The young man was of a serious mien and devoted all his waking hours to his music. He was well thought of by his masters and won several prizes and awards. He was particularly praised for his compositions and was happier composing than playing. His fellow students reveled in the gay abandon of Parisian society which was largely based on the cafes, bars and dance halls. Morrell found himself out of sympathy with the continental life style and resented not being able to make himself understood using the English language. Either his inability or his refusal to learn French resulted in many an explosive temper as he failed to make his meaning clear. Young ladies who heard him play were enchanted by his finesse, his sulky good looks and his head of tumbling curls and he was under no illusion about their desire for his company. However, he did not have the carefree manner and happy-go-lucky attitude of his *confréres* and his sullen moods soon put the ladies off any desire for further acquaintance.

He was pleased to leave the conservatoire at the age of 19 with many glowing testimonials and awards and gained the attention of a concert promoter who booked musicians for the various music societies that abounded all over France. Morrell played many concerts throughout greater Paris and was a popular attraction. To his disgust, however, he was seldom allowed to perform his own works and had to play a repertoire of familiar works by Mozart, Bach, Beethoven and other well-known composers.

On the strength of his concert successes in Paris he returned to London where he expected to make a profitable living as a soloist and composer. Unfortunately, he was now totally unknown in London, his three year absence severing any professional ties he may have established. Many months of idleness followed and he relied on the bounty of his parents who thought it was only a matter of time before he found his feet. Living in a garret in penury in a city where you are unseen is not conducive to the well being of any young man and he fell into bitter despair. He now started looking for any kind of musical work, eagerly chasing positions he had scorned a year earlier.

In 1901 he obtained the position of pianist in the Spa orchestra at Scarborough. This well known attraction in the town was resident for a long summer season from May to September playing every day in two different venues, one in the Royal Spa Hall and one in an outdoor arena. He stayed with a widowed lady called Mrs Miller in a cottage down a cobbled alley off Aberdeen Walk. Had he allowed himself, he could have enjoyed a healthy and enjoyable time walking on the cliffs and bathing in the sea as, even with rehearsals and performances, the schedule allowed of ample free time. But his morbid temperament seemed unable to permit him to enjoy life as other men and his air of permanent gloom did not endear him to his fellow musicians. In many of the concerts he was given the opportunity to play a piano solo but much to his chagrin, not only was he not allowed to play his own compositions, he was compelled to play such popular trifles as *The March of the Tin Soldiers* and similar *bagatelles*. Eventually this persistent disgruntled manner compelled the orchestra leader to dismiss him some weeks prior to the end of the season.

Back in London he retrieved some of his self-confidence and earned a fair amount of money by returning at the behest of his friend the French promoter to do a series of concerts. From this time on he established a routine of visiting Paris for a month each year during which he played many recitals and was treated with respect. The French promoter did not, of course, know that his protégé was not in demand elsewhere. The French payments kept him afloat while back home he eked out a living playing in various combinations of instruments in cafés and ball-rooms and playing for ballet rehearsals. For a while he toured the country accompanying a popular singer of sentimental ballads. This work, though torture to his acute sensibilities, did result in a hearty steady income for some months.

Morrell no longer despised playing for music societies

and several times played for the Baker Street Chamber Music Society, being prevailed upon to become a member himself. This he did at the persuasion of the society's president Lord Challis who engaged the young man every time he had a large function at Challis House. By this exposure to the aristocracy of London, Morrell found that other noble people would engage his services and he enjoyed mixing with his social superiors. However, when crossed he was still liable to be overcome with his uncontrollable temper. This was a great pity because in all other respects he was now a personable and handsome man and to certain ladies "devilishly attractive." ~ ~ ~

"Morello probably thought you were a prospective source of employment, Doctor," said Lord Challis with a smile.

"Then I will be a disappointment to him. My army pension does not permit the hiring of musicians. It's been very good to meet with you again, Lord Challis, Lady Challis, but I must return to my friend as it appears the concert is about to start."

"Perhaps we will see you again after the recital, Dr Watson? And perhaps meet your friend Mr Holmes again?" said Lady Challis.

"We will both look forward to it, Lady Challis," I replied giving a slight bow.

On returning to Holmes I told him his deduction regarding Lady Challis's leg was correct but he merely raised an eyebrow. I also told him of the brief meeting with the flamboyant young musician but that did not interest him either. I feared it was going to be a long evening and I bitterly regretted not settling for the usual half-pound of tobacco at Christmas. I looked at my watch which read eight o'clock; the concert should start at any moment and the chattering hub of the audience died down. It has always struck me how at all kinds of events without any sort of signal being given, the audience seems to spontaneously settle down and become quiet. Often, of course, it is a false alarm and the noise swells up again, as it did in this case. The audience, after settling to prepare itself for the silence ahead, suddenly became quite agitated and heads started craning round and straining upwards, a few men actually stood up and turned towards the doorway. There was a great scurrying and flurrying at the entrance and two people swept in – a prosperous hearty-looking gentlemen of about 45 and a lady who was recognised by the entire audience – with the sole exception of Mr Sherlock Holmes.

"I say, look who has just come in. That's Celia Norman the popular West End star."

The large hearty chap with the famous lady on his arm was being ushered into seats in the front row. They had the best view of the house as their seats were directly in front of the piano.


~ ~ ~ The girl child was the product of a solitary coupling between a laundress and a recruiting sergeant down a dark alley in the slums of Birmingham. Her mother named her Ami. The unusual spelling of the name Amy was a result of the ignorance of the laundress who was very ill-educated. One does not need much education to be a laundress. The name, however, turned out to be felicitous as the baby grew into a particularly friendly and loving little girl. All who came in contact with her liked her and she, herself, never saw evil in anybody.

Her mother being very poorly paid found it extremely difficult to keep body and soul together. In an attempt to find some security she married a man from the nearby foundry. Her scheme was somewhat thwarted by bearing seven more children over the years and the couple were dogged by continual penury. Ami was forced to do her share at the laundry and sometimes, unbeknownst to her mother, she would try on some of the customers clothing and dance about in it for fun. Eventually, to ease matters,

Ami was farmed out to an aunt of her mother who agreed to take the child at the age of eight as a sort of maid and companion. Ami had to work hard for her subsistence but she was a biddable girl and the aunt was very kindly disposed to her. As the two grew together the aunt became more like a grandmother to the growing girl teaching her to read and write as well as instructing her in many household tasks.

Ami's delight was to dance and the aunt encouraged her by enrolling her in a dancing school run by Madame Rubisova who claimed to have danced in the original production of *Swan Lake* in St Petersburg. As not many people in the suburb of Birmingham where Madame Rubisova held sway even knew where St Petersburg was, Madame Rubisova found it very easy to maintain her credentials and was never challenged on the fact that she had never been further than London or that she had been born, and remained, Elsie Roberts.

The dancing lessons were accompanied on the piano by a thin lanky youth called Malcolm who was in constant fear of Madame Rubisova and of losing his job which he relied on to supplement the meagre earnings he got from hawking wood and coal. Malcolm, although no more than a competent pianist himself, could still distinguish talent in others and reckoned that Ami was by far the cleverest girl of any age in the school. One day after the lesson he pulled Ami to one side and told her that he thought she was a swell dancer and he suggested that as he had a concertina they could go down into the better parts of the town and he could play while Ami danced. He reckoned that they would do well busking for the Saturday shoppers. Ami needed little persuading so that weekend they put their plan into operation.

There was no question that the public liked Ami's dancing but times were hard and not many people were prepared to put anything in the hat. They made a few coppers but that was only a start as Ami and Malcolm became a team and they turned not only to busking but went into pubs and bars, doing a turn and passing the hat. Ami knew her great-aunt would disapprove because she had pretentions of grandeur. Ami did not want to hurt the old lady's feelings but she wanted to get on. She was now thirteen and the wider world beckoned, unfairly fed by Malcolm's idealized vision of her rather ordinary talent.

The day came when Malcolm suggested they escape together and make for London. Like all young people since time out of mind he thought the opportunities in the metropolis were there for the mere picking-up. So the young couple made their way to the Great Wen.

They soon found that London was no different from Birmingham in that, whilst there were more people and more pubs, there were also a lot more struggling entertainers striving to earn a living – singers, musicians, acrobats, men escaping from chains, jugglers, all with their catchpenny antics. They found themselves renting the corner of a room from a Punch & Judy man and it was in this hovel that Ami would have given birth to her own child had not the services of a local "wise woman" procured an abortion. Even Ami could see Malcolm would be useless coping with a child. She had had a whole year of supporting him, keeping his resolve warm when he flagged, as he did more and more often. She realized that he was a handicap to her. Since reaching London she had seen many instances when she could better herself by allying herself elsewhere. She knew she was better-looking than most girls and she was not afraid of flashing her legs when she danced. She could do the splits and kick head high.

When she heard of somebody wanting girls for a dance troupe she went to the audition without telling Malcolm. Maurice Miller ran several troupes of girls that appeared all over the country and on the continent too. She was picked immediately on showing her prowess and told that she was to join a company going to Paris. She left four days later – without telling Malcolm.

Paris was an eye-opener for Ami. The entertainments there were much wilder than anything she had ever seen and some girls actually exposed their breasts in public. The Miller troupe was engaged in a respectable theatre in a musical comedy but after their show the girls would go to the Grand Véfour and the Elysée-Montmartre and see the riotous antics of the girls doing the *quadrille* which climaxed the evening's entertainment. When the Miller Girls returned to England Ami stayed on in Paris. She knew she could do the splits and kick as high as any of the *can-can* dancers in the *grand quadrille*. She was also far better looking as many of the stars of the *café-conc* were wildly eccentric in appearance and habits, so much so that they were known by nicknames – La Môme Fromage, Cigale and Grille d'Égout being some of the stars. She went to see M.Zidler the artistic director of the Moulin Rouge, the most famous of all the Montmartre dance halls, to try and persuade him to take her on. He agreed to give her a trial at no pay and she joined in the lesser stable of performers.

It was not a happy experience. She found that most of the girls worked for mere subsistence, many were hooked on absinthe and narcotics and not one of them welcomed an attractive English girl. The star was a lady known as La Goulue which meant "the Glutton" as she was notorious for draining other people's glasses dry in bars. Her rise to fame stemmed from her ability to high kick the top hat off customers' heads. She did not attempt to ingratiate herself with her public as Ami had been used to but showed an open contempt for them that they lapped up. She had a heart stitched on the back of her drawers which she would display at the end the *galop*. She would dance on the tables, swear like a trouper and would brook no upstart opposition. Managements trembled when she threatened to leave as she was their principal draw – wherever she chose to go, her public would follow. She was a law unto no-one but herself. The only interest she showed in her fellow *artistes* was an unhealthy one in the young woman known as The Cheese Kid.

Ami, soon realising that being amiable was not suffi-cient, retired back to more familiar territory. She met an Englishman called Victor who was a singer, *siffleur* and accordionist. He thought his act would be improved by the addition of a dancer and a female voice. He also thought his life would be improved by having a resident helpmate. They worked up an act and, returning to London, they scraped a living playing the meanest music halls. Ami knew she could not emulate the antics of the French *can-can* in England; it had been tried some years before and had been stopped by the police and the pro-prietor of the music hall fined. But they devised a pleasing diversion where Victor played excerpts from *Coppelia* accompanying himself whistling bird song while Ami danced gracefully all around in a manner that would not have aroused even the lustiest of men. However, what really drew the applause was when Victor donned a top hat and played a lively *tarantella* as Ami spun around him in a frenzied dance that culminated in kicking the hat off his head. They then exited to wild applause.

Going all round the country with this act they made a decent living earning £4 a week when working but still there were too many weeks out. One night after appearing at a crummy hall in the East End Ami was a handed a note which read "*Dear Madam, I saw your act this evening. You have great promise and are too talented to waste your time in your present occupation. If you would like to progress to the higher echelons of the theatre business please call and see me. I cannot do anything for your partner.*" It was signed Thaddeus Norman and his business card was enclosed. Mr Norman was one of a new breed of entrepreneur that had recently arisen. He was an artistes' agent. For many years performers had dealt directly with theatre managers but a few astute men realized that there was money to be made by being middle-men and they now facilitated contracts between management and artiste and, by doing so, managed to increase the pay of the performer.

She went to see Thaddeus Norman the very next day without telling Victor. As a result of her discussions she never went back to her partner. Mr Norman thought she had potential as a musical comedy star and proposed funding her for three months while she took singing and elocution lessons, had her hair styled, clothes made and instructed in the many things that Ami had never dreamed were necessary to be a star. She would not be paid during this time but would be housed in an apartment with all provided. When she protested she would be giving up £4 a week to do this, ignoring the fact her share was only half that, Mr Norman merely smiled and said that within a year she would be earning £50 a week.

When the three months had elapsed Mr Norman announced that he had got her a part in a witless trifle called *The Girl on Box Hill*. She was not the lead in this new musical comedy but had good opportunities and a solo number that Mr Norman thought could stop the show. Only one thing remained – her name. They had talked of this and many suggestions had been discarded; eventually they settled on Celia Norman. The first name they thought had the right balance between fun and res-pectability, the surname was easy because they were married at a small private ceremony in a country church at a village in Sussex where Mr Norman had a country home. Mr Norman was an astute man and sought to protect his investment.

Celia Norman caused a minor sensation in *The Girl on Box Hill* and from then on rapidly went from supporting artiste to star. She drew the public in show after show and, guided by her astute husband, her money climbed to £150 a week. Not only was she the most popular star on the musical comedy stage she was in great demand for advertising products and as a guest at social and charity functions. She now lived the lifestyle of a titled lady, albeit one who still had to work hard for a living. After too few years of this new life, shortly after the old Queen died, her husband also departed off this earth leaving everything to Celia.

The only difference this made to Celia was she no longer had to keep her lovers hidden or be circumspect about her peccadilloes. So her life carried on; she was by now, perhaps, not the biggest star in the West End firmament but she maintained her status and, more importantly, her salary. She was still beloved of her public and had no difficulty in receiving offers either of work or suitors. She still retained her air of amiability and only producers, certain theatre managers and her personal staff knew that inside she had a rod of steel that had been forged by La Goulue. ~ ~ ~

The chairman mounted the rostrum and called order by banging a gavel in the time honoured manner. "Ladies and Gentlemen, I welcome you to the January concert of the Baker Street Chamber Music Society. Regular members will know me by now as I have had the pleasure of being your chairman for four previous recitals. But for new members and guests who may not know me, permit me to introduce myself, I am Walter Porter from Whitechapel and, as well as being your chairman, it is my pleasure this evening to sing some songs which I hope will please and delight you." At this point a few persons thought it polite to offer up a smattering of applause. "We are about to start the concert but first, ladies and gentlemen, may I say we are very privileged to have with us this evening as our guest of honour the famous star of the West End stage Miss Celia Norman!"

This announcement was greeted with approval and hearty applause as Miss Norman and her escort rose to acknowledge the ovation and stepped up on to the dais.

"Good evening everyone! I'm so thrilled to be asked to come here tonight to your little musical soirée. After bringing delight to so many of you it is lovely for me to be able to sit and listen to other people providing the music. As many of you will know I am shortly to start rehearsals for my new show *The Beggar Princess* which will open next month at Daly's Theatre. It's a delightful musical comedy written by that wonderful composer Lionel Monckton. I play a poor beggar girl who turns out to be a princess. There are some beautiful new songs in it. I do hope to see you all there."

Miss Norman and her escort then stepped down and re-seated themselves while the audience applauded heartily.

"It is a great honour to welcome such an illustrious adornment of the West End stage to our humble musical entertainment. And you too, sir, are most welcome." Mr Porter bowed. "We are now ready to commence the concert. Later on we have a very famous star attraction – The Gloved Pianist. As you know, this gentleman hails from Italy and has captured the imagination of audiences all over the continent with his virtuoso playing whilst wearing white gloves. It is a great capture for us to have him with us tonight." Porter then consulted a paper in his hand and read "To commence the proceedings it is my pleasure to introduce your resident musicians the Baker Street Chamber String Quartet who will play a selection of pieces by Luigi Boccherini who was the royal composer to Friedrich Wilhelm II of Prussia. Boccherini died a hundred years ago this year and Mrs Adams the leader of the Baker Street Chamber String Quartet has spent some time searching for the music they are to play this evening. Please welcome Mrs Violet Adams and the Baker Street Chamber String Quartet."

Clad in some shapeless floating garment, a thin woman clutching a violin led the way on to the dais followed by her three colleagues, all male, with violin, viola and cello. We all applauded dutifully as they appeared, then waited patiently as they took an inordinate amount of time settling themselves down and arranging their chairs, bodies, instruments and music.

I dare not look at Holmes throughout all this farrago but I was well aware of him slumping lower in his seat. I must confess I had not realised that the Baker Street Chamber Music Society would be quite so inappropriate a place to thrust Holmes into. However, once the music started it sounded pretty much like the stuff I'd heard Holmes play on his fiddle so I thought he might perk up a bit. But even I could see that this evening was bound to be a bit of a come down after Kreisler.

After three or four short pieces from the quartet the chairman clambered on to the dais again and asked us to show our appreciation and we all applauded as they filed off the platform. Mr Porter then announced his accompanist on the lute, an earnest looking young man of about twenty-five who seated himself where he could gaze on the soloist. We then endured three old English folk songs, according to Mr Porter from Whitechapel, but whether it was his diction or he was singing in medieval language I know not, for I could not understand a word. But his extravagant gestures were entertaining and an occasional lack of cohesion between singer and lutenist caused open merriment from Miss Norman and her gentleman escort.

~ ~ ~ The city of Sheffield has been known for the manufacture of knives for hundreds of years. In Chaucer's *The Reeve's Tale*, written in the 1380s, he tells of the miller of Trumpington "*A Sheffeld thwitel baar he in his hose.*" (A long knife from Sheffield he carried in his hose.)

Until the mid-18th century knives were made from shear steel formed by forging bundles of blister steel but this process was rendered obsolete by the invention of crucible steel by Benjamin Huntsman in 1746. Demand for the new crucible steel grew dramatically, and Huntsman moved to a vast new site at Attercliffe – an area that became the main location for specialist steel making in Sheffield.

This new process advanced the steel manufacture of Sheffield to the first rank and, within 100 years, the town's factories were producing 20,000 tons of crucible steel per year, half the total European steel production. In 1801 46,000 people had lived in the area; by the death of Queen Victoria the population had risen to 409,000. 97% of the nation's cutlers were based in Sheffield, one of the most enterprising being Mr Hudson Shawcross.

Shawcross Ltd had been founded by Joseph Henry Shawcross who was born on 7 December 1830, in Sheffield. The young Shawcross was introduced to the steel making industry at the age of 9 by being sent to Thomas Turton & Sons where he was employed as a backer at a roller, taking out hot steel. His official hours were from 7am to 7pm but often he would work until 9 o'clock or even midnight. Sometimes he would have to start at 6 on Friday morning and not cease labour till 2 p.m. on Saturday. He would get some sleep in the dinner hour, and sometimes in the breakfast half hour, but was so tired he would fall asleep in working time waking up with a start when the hot steel came through. It was very heavy work lifting the steel as it emerged from the rollers and for this he earned four shillings a week.

Joseph Henry worked at several different jobs in the steel industry finally working, from the age of 18, at a small cutler's factory where he gleaned much knowledge of that specialized trade. In 1850, at the age of 20, learning of the gold strike in California, he voyaged to America with the intent of making his way to the California gold country. However, for some reason he initially settled in Pennsylvania and the following year in Illinois. In 1852, he journeyed across the Great Plains and Rocky Mountains to California. Within a year he struck lucky and was able to bank several hundred pounds. However, a couple of years later in 1855, not having made any further strikes, he travelled back to England.

Back in Sheffield he started up as a master cutler and

was soon considered one of the leading men of the town. He married in 1858 and his son Hudson was born a year later, rapidly followed by three daughters before his wife Sarah died in attempting to give birth to a further child. The grief at losing his wife affected him greatly and as a result he devoted inordinate care to the welfare and rearing of his only son.

Hudson was not a great scholar but a steady and dogged worker keeping out of trouble at the school run by the Rev Artemis Collins and emerging as a stolid but dependable youth of pleasant aspect. At the age of 13 he went to Rossall school in Lancashire where he thrived on Rev Robert Henniker's muscular Christianity precepts. This headmaster retired in 1875 to be replaced by Dr Herbert Armitage James who was considerably unpopular. Hudson Shawcross joined with his fellows outside the school to hiss and boo him at the end of his first year's headmastership. Contrary to their opinion the new head was, in fact, an inspired teacher raising the level of the school in all aspects and Hudson greatly benefitted from this during his final two years.

Returning home to Sheffield he entered his father's business, being made a partner on reaching the age of 25. Cutlers were in great demand, wages were high and workers had no problem getting jobs. Often it was the case that Hudson had to go searching the local pubs to round up his men. With strong beer at eight pints to the shilling, many preferred drinking to working. When he got them back to the factory the first thing they did was to try to wheedle what was termed "a sub" – an advance on the payment for a job – but Hudson Shawcross had learned the ways of working men and he was not to be trifled with; he would say "My father may fall soft but I'm not as green as I'm cabbage-looking." Neither was he complacent about the custom of "Saint Monday", the practice of utilizing the first day of the working week as a time for attending football matches when crowds of working men descended into what Hudson contemptuously called "tribal hooliganism".

1887 brought Queen Victoria's Golden Jubilee and Hudson was at the forefront of organising Sheffield's jubilations, persuading his fellow cutlers to give a day's holiday with full pay to all their workers. In the evening a huge bonfire and fireworks display took place and every child in the city was given a souvenir mug and a bun.

Shawcross Ltd leapt to the eminent place they currently hold via the success of their products at the Paris Exposition Universelle of 1889. Hudson was impressed by the main symbol of the Fair – a tower designed by M. Gustave Eiffel constructed of puddled iron, and the enormous Galerie des Machines which spanned the longest interior space in the world using a system of hinged arches designed to be constructed of steel but actually made in iron which was considerably cheaper. By now specialising in dainty cutlery and having an artistic designer on his staff, the exquisite fruit knives Shawcross Ltd displayed at the exhibition caught the fancy of the French wholesalers and orders poured in. This was the foundation of the firm's rapid expansion and diversification into many and varied fine steel products.

Hudson married in 1890 and had a house built in the countryside outside Sheffield. He stated he did not want his children brought up in the stinking vile atmosphere of the city. Driving a pony and trap he would set off for his factory at 8am each morning returning at 6pm to take dinner with his wife and family. In 1894 he bought his first motor car, a very neat Benz Velo of 1½ horse power. He was very interested in powered machines changing his vehicles frequently as such transport improved rapidly during the last days of the 19th century and into the present decade. This go-ahead business man is also very much a family man presently having four children who eagerly await Papa's return in his motor car.

Tragedy struck this benign cutler when his father

Joseph Henry Shawcross shot himself on 23 November 1895. Having recently retired from active participation in Shawcross Ltd he had lived a melancholy life at his large house in Fulwood Road accompanied by his sole unmarried daughter. It appears he never got over the death of his wife and did the deed on the same day that his wife died. The verdict of the coroner's jury was "Suicide while temporarily insane." His real and personal estate was proved at some £85,000 which he left in its entirety to his spinster daughter Ada. ~ ~ ~

By now Holmes was becoming very restless and, never amused by inefficiency of any kind, musical or otherwise, was looking round, presumably seeking a way to make his exit. However we were in the middle of a row and even Holmes's notorious brusqueness would have been unconscionably rude at this point as the chairman was now introducing the next artiste.

"And now we come to the star of the evening – a musician of extraordinary talent who has set all of Europe aflame. I first saw this talented pianist at an *al fresco* concert in Folk-es-ton. Please welcome Signor Guido Salvato – the Gloved Pianist!" with a flourish of his upraised hand in the direction of the door, the chairman stepped off the rostrum leaving the way for Signor Salvato to progress to the piano.

The Signor was a small man with curly hair and a neat beard. He seated himself at the piano and flourished his hands in the air displaying his immaculate white gloves. The audience was hushed as raising his hands he brought them down on to the keyboard to play several resounding opening chords. He then did an extraordinary thing: leaping to his feet he let out an awesome cry, thrust his hands into his armpits and fell to the ground with a crash sending the piano stool flying. Several things then happened simultaneously – the audience gasped in alarm, Holmes instantly moved from inert indifference to alert tension and the chairman rushed forward and crouched over the crumpled body now slumped on the floor.

Shortly he rose and spoke. "I fear he has collapsed. I am very sorry, ladies and gentlemen, but Signor Salvato seems to have been taken ill. Is there a doctor in the house?"

Naturally I immediately rose to my feet. "I'm a doctor! John H Watson, late Indian Army."

"Oh, sir, if you would be so good as to come forth," cried the chairman.

I had no medical equipment with me, of course, but after turning Salvato on to his back it only took a look to see that the man was dead. I thrust my hand inside his boiled shirt but of a heartbeat there was no vestige. I turned to the chairman who was hovering anxiously by.

"I'm afraid Signor Salvato is dead."

"Dead? How can this be?" protested the worried chairman.

"Probably a heart attack – I have no medical equipment with me, I cannot examine him properly. Good God!" I cried as I looked down at the recumbent pianist.

"What is it?"

"Look at his hands!" I stooped and lifted a wrist – the glove was covered in blood, as was the one on his other hand. "They are covered in blood! What has happened?" I rose again and looked at the piano in bewilderment. There must be something that caused the man to bleed. I was just about to inspect the keys when I heard a shout.

"Watson! Don't touch the keyboard!" Holmes had risen and pushed his way forward.

"What is this? I do not understand! Who are you, sir?" demanded Mr Porter the chairman.

"This is Mr Sherlock Holmes, the famous detective," said I and a great murmuring arose in the audience. Holmes's name was well known, his reputation had been growing for over twenty years. Instantly he took charge

"I must examine this man. Touch nothing! Nobody must leave this hall. You, sir, how many exits are there from this room?"

The chairman looked petrified as he tried to grasp the import of Holmes question. "There is the one we all entered by and that one there which is an emergency exit." He indicated a door halfway along one wall.

"Where does that door lead?" snapped Holmes.

"It opens to a narrow passage that leads directly to Bond Street," replied the man.

"Get a couple of strong fellows and station them at that exit and alert the two men at the entrance. They are to prevent anybody from leaving. Forcibly if necessary. Go on, man, don't just stand staring!"

"Yes, yes, of course." He hurried out muttering to himself.

Holmes saw the lute player, clutching his instrument, pressed up against a pillar. "Ah my good fellow, do you think you could play some pleasant music while I carry out my examination? Ladies and gentlemen, this is a most unusual position in which you find yourselves. I am afraid I must ask you to remain calm and seated whilst I determine the course of action. Please be so good as to listen to this young gentleman. Please play something whilst I examine this man."

Holmes produced the pocket lens that he was never without and was not long in his examination. He beckoned me down to his side and quietly spoke. "Watson, when you examined the man's hands did you notice a tattoo on the inside of the wrist?"

"I did but I did not remark it."

"Take a close look."

On the inside of the man's arm just above the wrist was a device with two letters entwined, a C and an N. Holmes held out a glove covered in blood that he had removed from the maestro's hand. "And what do you make of that, Watson?"

"Good heavens, Holmes, the fellow's gloves have several cuts. What does this mean?"

"It means that this innocent looking musical instrument is in fact a deadly weapon. Stand clear, Watson."

Holmes produced a pair of manicure tweezers and most carefully, grasping the tweezers through a folded handkerchief, gingerly went along the keyboard depressing one key after another. "Your handkerchief, Watson. Lay it on top of the piano." I did as he bade. Every so often, with the tweezers, he plucked from between the keys a small rectangle of metal which he laid on my handkerchief with the utmost care.

"What are they Holmes? They look like tiny knives. Diabolical!" I breathed.

"I fancy these are the new invention of the American Mr King Camp Gillette."

"New invention?"

"A new type of razor to enable gentlemen to shave in safety."

"I've never heard of such a thing. They don't look very safe to me."

The gentleman who was the escort to Miss Celia Norman, witnessing Holmes's procedure from his chair immediately in front of the piano, leaned forward and spoke. "If I may make so bold as to interrupt you, Mr Holmes. You are correct. Indeed they are disposable razor blades. I have heard of your reputation and we are indeed fortunate to have you here at the very time the murder was committed."

"You say 'murder', sir?" asked Holmes.

"Well, yes. It would seem to be that someone has chosen this bizarre method to kill Signor Salvato the gloved pianist," replied the escort.

"One might see that a malicious person, a jealous rival, perhaps, may wish to damage a musician's hands in this manner but why do you say murder?"

"The man's dead, isn't he?"

"True, but perhaps the shock of slashing his fingers caused a heart attack."

"Then the malicious person you speak of has caused more damage then he intended." The gentleman spoke with a Yorkshire accent and had the forthright manner of many men from that county.

"I play Devil's Advocate. You are correct. It is certainly murder." Holmes leant over the blades reposing on my handkerchief and smelled them. "These blades have been dipped in a deadly poison – a type of curare. A poison in which the Amazonian Indians dip their arrows before putting them in their blowpipes. This poison is so potent that the tiniest amount on an open wound is instant death. The pianist had no chance – as soon as his finger was cut the poison entered his system and stopped his breath. The man died from asphyxia. It seems significant that you immediately assumed the death was murder. Tell me about these blades, sir, you seem to know about them."

"I should do – I manufacture them."

"Indeed?" said Holmes in surprise.

"My name is Hudson Shawcross. I have a factory in Sheffield that turns out all manner of small goods in fine steel."

"You realise, sir, that by admitting to being a maker of these things you are putting yourself under great suspicion," pointed out Holmes.

"Nonsense, sir! Mr King Camp Gillette invented this system to ease gentlemen's shaving. They came into use in the USA last year and now they have come to Britain. As you will know, whatever America does first we Britons follow. I have Mr Gillette's licence to manufacture his product here. So it's no more of the old cut-throat razor – we chaps can now use these disposable blades in a safety holder that bends the flexible blade to the right angle, and bob's your uncle. They are not yet on sale in this country, but prototypes have been widely distributed. And any fellow who has travelled to America could have brought some back with him. So no more expensive trips to the barber and no more the hazard of nicking your own face."

"So these things will be on general sale?" asked Holmes.

"Very shortly, sir, in packets of five blades. The holders are available separately. I don't have the rights for making those."

"Thank you, Mr Shawcross for your explanation. I am much in your debt. It is clear that these blades were placed between the piano keys prior to the performance."

The chairman returned to Holmes. "Mr Holmes I have two men at both doors and they know what to do if anybody tries to leave the building. I have also sent for an ambulanza."

"Excellent, you have done well. Though I am afraid that will only serve to take this poor fellow to the morgue. I must ask you also to send a message to Scotland Yard summoning a police detective to come as soon as possible. To Scotland Yard mind, a local bobby will be of no use. Say that Sherlock Holmes requires assistance at the Grafton Gallery in Bond Street immediately."

"I will do so at once, Mr Holmes. Mrs Adams the leader of the string quartet wishes to speak to you," said the chairman leading that lady forward before hastening off to do Holmes's bidding.

"May I speak, sir?" asked Mrs Adams in a breathless undertone.

"Of course," said Holmes kindly.

The violinist looked around nervously. "I saw you pulling those nasty things out of the keyboard. I can definitely say that those things were not on the piano when my quartet tuned our instruments."

"When was that?"

"Right up to the time the audience started coming in."

"You are sure of that?"

"Most definitely. We were rehearsing right up to the time the doors were opened to permit the entrance of the audience. Even as the first arrivals were seating themselves I was hastily putting the bandstand in order and the last thing I did was to check the keyboard and give it a final dusting. To have it perfect for our star guest. I could not have missed seeing several metal blades. I am certain of that."

Holmes turned and stared at the audience still supposed to be listening to the faltering efforts of the lute player but actually craning their necks and straining their ears to ascertain what the great detective had found out. Turning to me Holmes muttered in my ear. "That is most significant. This means that the murderer must have placed the razor blades between the keys after the time of the first arrivals and before the beginning of the concert. Ask that fellow to stop torturing his lute would you, Watson."

The lute player was relieved to obey my request and mopped his face. Holmes had no need to call the audience to attention as they were silent and rapt and waited to hear his every word. "Ladies and gentleman, I must take you into my confidence. There is no doubt at all that before your very eyes a murder has taken place here tonight. The means are novel and diabolical. The pianist cut his hands on razor blades that had been dipped in a deadly poison originating in the native tribes of the Amazon basin. I now must ask you all to search your minds and answer me a most important question. Did anyone see any person approach the piano prior to the start of the concert?"

There was much consternation at the mention of the word 'murder' and the sinister method of carrying it out. Holmes's question started members of the audience debating amongst themselves until a patrician voice rang out.

"Yes, Mr Holmes, I saw such a man!"

"Ah, Lord Challis, I am pleased to renew our acquaintance. I trust you and your lady are well?"

Lord Challis turned and addressed the audience. "You all know me I have been the President of this Society since it was founded eighteen years ago. I say to you that Mr Sherlock Holmes is the most brilliant man in the art of detection and we could not have a better man here on the spot to solve this crime. Mr Holmes was responsible for finding my son when he disappeared in mysterious circumstances. I say all this so that you will put your trust in Mr Holmes and answer his questions honestly and fearlessly."

"Thank you for those kind words, Lord Challis. Now can you tell us who it was that approached the piano prior to the concert?"

"I can. We were the very first to enter the room to-night. We were early. I find my chauffeur needs less time for the journey by motor car than my coachman did with a pair of horses. We were in the foyer for fully twenty minutes before the doors to the hall were opened to us. We could hear the quartet rehearsing then, when they ceased, the door was thrown open and we were permitted to enter. I assure you we were the first to be seated. As you can see we have an uninterrupted view and I saw a man step up on to the platform and start fiddling about with the music on the piano. I thought he was part of Signor Salvato's entourage for tonight, probably acting as his page turner – "

"Page turner!" A man leaped to his feet howling the words in derision. "You insult me, sir. The meanest gut-tersnipe is too good to be a page turner for that black-guard!" The speaker was a handsome enough looking man of about twenty-five with a mass of black tumbling locks. Dressed, like all the men present, in evening dress he differed only by sporting a waistcoat of patterned brocade. He was the young man who had butted in when I was conversing with Lord and Lady Challis.

"May I ask your name sir?" asked Holmes.

"My name is Aubrey Morello. I am known to most

of the members here as I am a pianist and composer of some repute and have performed for this Society."

"Mr Morrello is one of our most distinguished members, Mr Holmes. He often performs in Parigi where his works are well known," gushed the chairman.

"Neither the name or the face are known to me. Mr Morello, perhaps you would tell us why you approached the piano when you are here not as a performer but a mere member of the audience?"

"There is no mystery, sir. I went to examine the programme to be played by that charlatan the so called Gloved Pianist."

"Were you not content to wait like the rest of us, to see what – er, delights were in store?"

"I wanted to be sure he was not intending to play any of my works," replied Morello tossing his abundant curls.

"I see. You did not want him to do that?"

"Certainly not! The man is nothing but a low class music hall performer masquerading as a classical pianist."

"You may well be right, Mr Morello, but I take it from the vehemence of your reply that you did not like the man for stronger reasons that his status in the musical profession."

"I hated him! I have hated Salvato since we were fellow students at the Paris Conservatoire," spat out Morello.

"What is the reason for this hatred?" asked Holmes urbanely.

"The reason is simple, Mr Holmes. He was a gross, idle, useless fellow – a deplorable musician as a student and still the same now. When he was studying, Salvato scraped by doing the minimum of work, narrowly avoiding being thrown out on his ear. Just because he was Italian he was favoured by the professors most of whom were Italian or French. Whereas because I was an Englishman they never considered my talents. The musical snobs do not think the English are musical."

"Morello does not appear to be an English name?"

"It is a stage name," confessed Morello. "My true name is Morrell. I added the O to give the impression I was Italian. The English musical snobs don't think the English are musical either. Salvato never even graduated yet, by means of this stupid ploy of playing the piano with white gloves on, somehow he had managed to persuade people he was a star pianist. Whereas I, who graduated with the highest honours, won the Mozart prize for composition, a distinction in conducting, am compelled to a hand to mouth existence."

"But the chairman told us you have a distinguished career in Paris. How can you now tell us you live in penury?" asked Holmes.

"Well perhaps I exaggerate when I say that, but my means are modest and, whilst my compositions are highly regarded, there is little money in original work. I am very prolific and I have written many pieces that still wait for their first performance. Unfortunately since music lovers prefer to hear the music they know we have endless recitals of Chopin, Bach and Beethoven while new work such as mine languishes unplayed."

"I see. Well you have made your position very clear, Mr Morello. However, by confessing your long-held hatred you have placed yourself in a position of deep suspicion. How do we know you did not take the opportunity to rid yourself of this man you so hated by placing razor blades between the keys? An act easily and swiftly done while you purported to riffle through the music book?"

"Though I wished the blackguard dead, I was not the hand that did the deed. Where would I obtain a deadly poison known only to the Amazon Indians?"

"In matters of this nature we cannot simply take your word, sir. Anyone in the hall could have used this dastardly method of murder."

"Of course, sir. But if I wanted to kill the man would I not just shoot him? Or bludgeon him to death on a dark night? Would I contrive this bizarre public death for a man I hate? But if I am the murderer it is for you to prove my guilt, not for me to prove my innocence."

"I am well versed in the law of the land, sir. You may sit down. No doubt I shall need to question you further."

The bumptious musician swaggered back to his seat and Holmes once more addressed the audience. "Ladies and gentlemen, you have been very patient and I fear my investigations may take some time. Watson, will you kindly organise someone to assist you in taking the body out of the hall to the foyer? Perhaps a discreet place or cover may be found there until the ambulance arrives. Once again I ask if anybody else was seen to approach the piano. I must ask you to think hard and carefully. Did you see anyone else near the piano prior to the start of the concert?" Like the Roman of old he paused for a reply and I, with the help of the chairman and another man, carried the corpse out of the hall.

When I returned I found to my astonishment that the audience was no longer seated but people were mingling about, chatting earnestly to one another and some idly looking at the rather odd pictures on the walls. Holmes emerged from the door from which Salvato had made his entrance.

"Well done, Watson. Please come in here." I found myself in a small room that was obviously in use as the dressing room for the artistes appearing in the concert. With Holmes was Edmund Redvers-Gordon. "We cannot expect the people to sit rigidly but, as yet, we cannot let anyone go. Nobody has volunteered that they saw any other person approach the piano but I think you will agree that this gentleman did indeed do so. You, yourself, pointed him out to me as a face that was known to you."

"Are you not Edmund Redvers-Gordon the well-known explorer?

"I am indeed, Dr Watson."

"Since taking my seat I observed two people approach the piano. Most people see but do not observe. I have trained my faculties so that I not only see but observe as well. The two persons were Mr Morello, from whom we have just heard out in the hall, the other is – you, sir," said Holmes sternly.

"I have heard of your reputation, Mr Holmes. I should have known I could not escape your eagle eye," replied the explorer with a wry smile.

"I understood from the newspapers that you had recently left for Darkest Africa," I ventured.

"Indeed I should have been arriving in Matabeleland as we speak but just before my departure I heard that my source of funding had been abruptly withdrawn. I was all ready to leave when I had a message to say that the bankers' draft I was expecting would not be sent. Without the funds I could not contemplate leaving. I am trying to raise money elsewhere, my expedition is now pending but if I do not get money from somewhere the thing will shortly fall apart."

"How unfortunate. It seems most unkind and unorthodox to leave you in the lurch like that at the last minute," said I sympathetically.

"You put it most politely, sir. I regret my reaction was far more intemperate."

"Do you mind disclosing the source of your funding and why it was so precipitately withdrawn?" asked Holmes.

"It's no secret. Mr Holmes. It has been in the papers. The Andrew Carnegie Foundation suddenly changed its policy. It decided to increase its work with arts and music. Apparently they think it more important to support a well-established culture sufficiently able to look after itself rather than help me explore the unknown recesses of the Dark Continent. Hence this music society is able to afford to engage a star of the calibre of the Gloved Pianist."

"I see. So are you a member of this society?"

"No, Mr Holmes. Music does not have particular

charms for me. I came as the guest of a friend specifically to see – to see – the sort of thing that the Carnegie Foundation is supporting. I feel very keenly the withdrawal of support from my expedition."

"Have you ever been to South America, Mr Redvers-Gordon?"

"Yes, Mr Holmes. I have spent some time in that continent."

"Perhaps you are familiar with the Amazon region?"

"I am, and my discoveries there have led to increased knowledge of the area. I venture to suggest that much of what you may know of the region is as a result of my endeavours."

"Does the term 'velvet leaf' mean anything to you?"

"It does."

"Perhaps you would explain it to Dr Watson? As a medical man he has interest in such things."

"Velvet leaf is a term the Witoto tribe of the Amazon forest use to describe a poisonous concoction."

"Do you wish to elaborate?" asked Holmes.

"It is a deadly poison made from the bark of *strychnos toxifera* mixed with *chrondrodendron tomentosum* to form a curare made even more virulent by the incorporation of toad and snake venom. The Witoto boil this mess for two days. The result is the most insidious poison known to man. It is harmless if ingested by swallowing but, if it enters the blood stream via an open gash or wound, death is instantaneous. The Witoto dip their arrow tips in the stuff so that the slightest hit piercing the skin will be a deadly one."

"Am I correct when I say the poison causes apnea – the cessation of breath?" asked Holmes.

"You are correct, sir."

"Thank you, you have summoned up the cause of the man's death very succinctly. Perhaps it is possible that you have brought some of this poison back home with you?"

"I bring many native artefacts back with me. Part of

the purpose of my expeditions is to bring hidden things back to the wider world; but I do not have such poison."

"Perhaps you would be so kind to tell us why you took such an interest in the piano when you entered the room?"

"That is easily explained. A colleague of mine who is resident in Africa wished me to arrange the delivery of a piano to him. As you must know the climate in the tropics is very hot and very humid. They are terrible conditions for a piano. I have said I am not a music lover. I was merely looking at the piano with an interest as to how it would survive both the climate and the shipping. That is all."

"Thank you, you have been most co-operative."

"I have no reason not to be."

"You will see my quandary, Mr Redvers-Gordon. It would seem that nobody approached the piano except you and Mr Morello. The leader of the resident quartet assures us that the piano was free of razor blades when she inspected it as the members entered."

Redvers-Gordon shrugged "Perhaps you should question Mr Morello more stringently."

"Holmes, one of the two must be the criminal," I cried.

"Watson, are you seriously suggesting that one man should kill another for the trivial reason that the funding for his expedition has been withdrawn? Or that in the other case Mr Morello has killed a rival through professional jealousy?"

"You of all people, Holmes, know that when a man broods on what he perceives to be an injustice he may be tempted to any kind of wickedness."

"I must correct you, Mr Holmes. I do not regard the funding of my expedition as trivial. However I am thankful to say that the Royal Geographical Society has consented to make up the deficiency. I shall be leaving tomorrow morning."

"Indeed?   You are to leave tomorrow morning yet you spend your last night before departure at a recital of a music society of which you are not even a member?  A man who professes he is not a music lover?   Come, sir. You must have much more important matters to attend to."

"I see it is hopeless trying to fool you, Mr Holmes. Very well.  I came to see a certain lady.  I am leaving this country for ever.  I do not intend to return ever again.  My heart has been broken.  I intend to spend the rest of my life buried in my work."

"I see; the real reason for your presence here is nothing to do with your funding difficulties but to say farewell to a certain lady?"

"Not even that.  I did not hope to speak.  Merely to take away a last vision of my beloved."

"I do not think there are any unaccompanied ladies here tonight, sir," said I.

"Oh, she is accompanied all right.  But I expected her to be with her new paramour, not on the arm of Hudson Shawcross."

"These are deep waters.  You say you did not expect to see Miss Celia Norman with Mr Shawcross. With whom did you expect to see her?"

"With Guido Salvato, the Gloved Pianist."

"Do you mean to say that Miss Norman broke off with you to have a liaison with the man who is now dead?" asked Holmes with some incredulity.

"She did.  I thought she loved me as passionately as I loved her but I was sadly mistaken.  She thought a famous explorer would be exciting but she found me dull.  Celia Norman is a woman who craves bright lights, mindless folly, and superficial people.  She found all those things with Salvato – a man as brainless as she.  Yet I am in thrall to her beauty, I cannot deny it.  I came for a last glimpse of a lost love but those feelings are stirring in me again at the very sight of her.  Her very presence ensnares me.  I cannot wait to leave the country. Have you finished with me?"

"For the moment, but I must ask you to remain in the hall. No one can be permitted to leave at present."

"I understand, Mr Holmes." The explorer left the room to rejoin the throng in the hall.

"Well, Holmes, I did not expect Celia Norman to be that sort of woman," said I somewhat disappointed.

Holmes gave a short laugh, "Hah, Watson! You and your chivalry. All women are the same, some more devious than others, but all out to get what they can from men."

"I say, Holmes, the CN device tattooed on Salvato's arm – Celia Norman!"

"You think Salvato was so enamoured of Miss Norman he had the tattoo done as some kind of love token?"

"It is just the sort of thing a Latin gigolo would do. You will have to interview Miss Norman, I think."

"Of course. What is it?" Holmes turned as the chairman entered.

"Mr Holmes, there is a gentleman here wishes to speak with you." He stood aside to permit a small stout man to enter.

"You wish to see me, sir?"

"Yes, Mr Holmes. I have just been speaking to Lord Challis out there and he said I must come and tell you."

"Tell me what, sir?"

"Some time ago I went to play chess with Edmund Redvers-Gordon. The famous explorer. He is here to-night. In his library he showed me a glass phial which he said contained something he called Velvet Leaf. He said it was a deadly poison from South America so when you told us about the blades dipped in a similar poison I thought I should inform you of this incident."

"You did correctly, sir. Mr Redvers-Gordon has just informed us that he does not possess such poison."

"Well he certainly did then, Mr Holmes. I had never

~ 72 ~

heard of such stuff and cautioned him to keep it safely locked away if it was as virulent as he claimed."

"You must challenge him on this, Holmes," I cried.

"Where was this phial, sir?"

"As I said, in his library. It was more like a museum. His house is crammed full of artefacts and objects from all over the world. After every expedition he brings back many many things."

"Thank you sir, please give your name to Dr Watson here and rejoin the others."

"Well, Holmes," I said when we were alone again, "it begins to look at though the explorer is our man."

"Possibly. Perhaps you would be so kind as to ask Mr Redvers-Gordon what he has to say in response to the accusation that he showed his chess opponent a phial containing Velvet Leaf. Then you could bring Miss Celia Norman back here."

When I re-entered the hall it was clear that the members had become much more relaxed. Now the body had been removed from their sight and Holmes was also absent they had settled into a conventional social atmosphere and were chatting as though nothing uncommon had taken place, much less a macabre murder. I found Redvers-Gordon sitting with another man, presumably the member with whom he had arrived.

"I am sorry to interrupt your conversation, gentlemen, but Mr Holmes has instructed me to put another question to Mr Redvers-Gordon."

"Fire away, Dr Watson," replied the explorer breezily.

"Perhaps it would be better asked in private," said I indicating discreetly the presence of his companion.

"I've no secrets from anybody, Dr Watson, especially my dear chum Porky. I repeat – ask away."

"Very well. We have received intelligence that when a gentleman visited your house to play chess you showed him a phial containing a poison and stated it was called Velvet Leaf. What do you have to say to that, sir?"

"I do not have any such poison now. Perhaps it was some time ago when this unnamed gentlemen visited my house."

"So you did have some at one time? What happened to it?"

Redvers-Gordon shrugged "I regret to say I do not know."

"That seems an unsatisfactory reply," said I in incredulity, "to be so careless with a deadly poison."

"You must understand, doctor, my house is a treasure trove of artefacts and wonders from all over the world. None of these objects is catalogued and I have so much stuff I do not know the half of what I've got."

"And that is all you have to say?"

"That is all I can say. I know nothing more of the night when I played chess nor nothing more of the fatal deed tonight."

With that I gave a stiff bow and left this strange man. How odd that a man who has braved dangers all over the world, who has risked death and disease in many forms to explore the unknown reaches of this planet should have lost his heart to a faithless woman and yet remain so calm and controlled. Of course I do not go along with Holmes's assessment of women. My dear late wife was a treasure and, as are most wives, loyal to me in every respect. Perhaps if Holmes finds the love of a good woman he will alter his severe opinions of the fair sex. Although he is not getting any younger, time is not on his side.

I approached Miss Norman without enthusiasm. If it were true about her *affaire* with Salvato, and we certainly knew of her dalliance with Redvers-Gordon, and it was clear from her demeanour that her present escort Hudson Shawcross was more than just a friend, that made three liaisons we knew of concerning men present that night! How many others had there been?

"Miss Norman, I am Sherlock Holmes's friend and

messenger. He requests you will come with me to the room behind the stage where he has some questions he would like to ask you."

"How thrilling! Come along Hudson, I am to be 'grilled' as they call it in America."

"I think Mr Holmes would prefer to speak with you alone, Miss Norman."

"I'm sure he would, most men do," she replied with a coquettish leer.

"I insist on being present, otherwise Miss Norman will not comply," announced Shawcross pompously.

So we all trouped off to where Holmes awaited us. I was stopped by the chairman who said the ambulance was here and was it all right for the body to be taken. I assured him there was no more we could glean from the corpse and the men should take it straight to the morgue.

"Ah, come in, Miss Norman and you too Mr Shawcross. I have some questions for you Miss Norman, of a personal nature. You may prefer to give your answers in confidence."

"Is Dr Watson staying?"

"He is. You can trust his discretion."

"Then Mr Shawcross stays too," smiled Miss Celia Norman.

"As you wish," agreed Holmes with a slight incline of his head. "We have been told by Mr Redvers-Gordon that you were his paramour. Have you anything to say to this, Miss Norman?"

"Only that I thought I associated with gentlemen."

"Come, madam, I think we need to know a little more," said Holmes sternly.

"What do you want me to say? Yes, it's true that Edmund and I were lovers. It's also true that he is the most boring man on earth. Every time I visited his home he showed me these trinkets and souvenirs that he had brought back from some God-awful place."

"These trinkets etc. Did he ever show you a phial of

poison from the Amazon?"

"He might have. I don't remember." She paused. "There were so many things. You think it was Edmund who brought that vile stuff here tonight that killed Guido?"

"He says not and you cannot remember ever seeing such a thing in his house. Pray continue."

"Well he was always so serious. His idea of a good night out was to listen to a Christian missionary talk about converting the heathen in China. A girl wants something a bit more exciting than that."

"So you took up with Signor Salvato the Gloved Pianist?"

"Yes. He swept me off my feet. I couldn't resist Guido's Italian charm. He took me to Venice and Rome, the opera in Milan. We went to Sicily to meet his family. He introduced me to his brothers. We had a wonderful time."

"But you have not stayed with him, Miss Norman?"

"No. You know how it is, Mr Holmes. A new passion sweeps you off your feet and you are deliriously in love. Then you get to know each other better and you find out more about your beloved and love starts to wane. What at first seem delightful traits become a source of annoyance. Guido was very self-centred, he expected the world to revolve round him. At first I admired his self assurance but I soon realised that it was actually selfish arrogance. He expected me to dance to his tune. Celia Norman is not at any man's beck and call!"

"So you parted?"

"We did. Not without some regrets I have to say, but you know how it is, Mr Holmes."

"I regret I do not, Miss Norman."

Any further questions were forestalled by the door crashing open and Aubrey Morello bursting in in a towering rage.

"I will kill this woman!" he cried. Holmes and I had

to forcibly restrain him.

"Aubrey! Don't make a fool of yourself! You are nothing in all this!" snapped Celia Norman.

"I? Nothing? I who have been reduced to poverty through lavishing gifts on you? Nothing?" screamed Morello beside himself with anger.

"What is all this?" asked Shawcross in bewilderment.

"This – this harpy was the lover of that – that imposter of a musician. I have just been speaking to Redvers-Gordon the explorer. He has told me all about you and that scoundrel. All my life he has thwarted me – as students he crowed over me, as pianists he has lorded it over me with his pathetic antics and now I find he has also stolen my woman. It is insufferable! All the time you were supposed to be with me you were two-timing with that – that – apology of a musician!"

"I got you a job as rehearsal pianist for my next show, what more do you want?" said Celia Norman coolly.

"I will kill her!" stormed Morello.

"I am sure you have been sorely used Mr Morello," said Holmes,"but there has been serious violence done here tonight. Do not add to it."

Morello ceased his struggle and we relaxed our grip on him.

"I'm sorry." He slumped in a chair his head in his hands. He was a picture of a man in abject despair.

"Well, Miss Norman, it seems that I am at the end of quite a long line," said Hudson Shawcross.

"Don't be silly, darling, you knew I wasn't exactly chaste. They were mere peccadilloes, darling. You know it is you whom I truly love."

"Do I? I think at the time you gave that impression to the other fellows too."

"Oh, darling, would I pretend to you?" said Miss Norman stroking his arm with a show of affection.

"Well I suppose not," muttered the mollified steel magnate.

I think I was the only one in the room aware of the slight sound that emanated from Holmes. A sound that is usually rendered in print as "Harrumph!" Holmes gave permission for Miss Norman and Mr Shawcross to return to the hall then turned his attention to Morello who was still sitting in his dejection.

"Well, Mr Morello, you have had a rude awakening. You will now see that your dalliance has proved not only expensive but fruitless."

"I've been a fool. I see that now. I'm sorry to have made such a public ass of myself." He stumbled to his feet and brusquely pushed past leaving the two of us alone.

"This is a pretty kettle of fish, Holmes. The late Signor Salvato seems to have been involved with several people who might have wished his death."

"You have been making notes, Watson. Please to read them out so that we may clarify the situation."

"Certainly, Holmes. We have four people involved in this death in some way. Miss Celia Norman was the paramour of them all. Mr Redvers-Gordon has had his heart broken and is leaving the country. Mr Morello has been reduced to poverty and cast aside. Both these gentlemen were thrown over in favour of Guido Salvato the Gloved Pianist who is the murdered man. Mr Shawcross is her present beau. We know Salvato met his death by the dastardly means of razor blades and poison. We know both Redvers-Gordon and Morello had access to the piano. Mr Shawcross is the manufacturer of these new-fangled razor blades. Mr Redvers-Gordon admits to having possessed a deadly poison of the type used. Miss Norman could well have obtained possession of this poison unbeknownst to Mr Redvers-Gordon. Mr Morello admits that he has had a life-long hatred for the dead man."

"Well done, Watson. In your usual inimitable manner you have honed directly in on the nub of the problem."

There was a hammering on the closed door of the

room.  When I opened it I found a very flustered Mr Walter Porter the chairman.  "Could one of you come to the foyer, please?"

"Can you go, Watson?  My mind is engaged on the present problem."

I left the bustling chairman as he was waylaid by queries from his members as to what exactly was happening. In the foyer I found a very angry large man.  He was aged about fifty, dressed smartly but not in evening clothes. Round his neck on a black ribbon was a pair of *pince-nez*. Dithering around him making ineffectual noises was the ancient secretary who had issued me with the subscription prior to Christmas

"What the devil is going on here?  Why am I being prevented from entering the gallery?" the large man thundered.

"May I explain?" started I when he interrupted  "I would be much obliged if you did so.  Who the devil are you for a start?"

"My name is Dr John Watson.  The Chamber Music Society of Baker Street is holding a recital here tonight –"

"I know that, man!  I hire out the room and provide the piano!"

The secretary, successfully raising his voice above a pathetic bleat, informed me that the angry gentleman was the manager of the Grafton Galleries.

"Ah," said I, realising that this man was not a press reporter as I had at first mistakenly assumed. "The very man I wanted to see. I did not realise you were on the premises," I continued, thinking quickly of some way to appease him.

"I was in my office catching up on my accounts. Then before going home I thought I would call in and see half an hour or so of the concert.  I invariably slip in at the back on a Chamber Music night.  Tonight when I tried to do that these two men here prevented me!  They actually interposed their bodies between me and the door!  My door! The door to my own gallery! I repeat, doctor, what the devil is going on here tonight?"

"If you would calm yourself, sir, I can explain." Glancing at the two sturdy committee men, who on the chairman's instructions had barred entry as well as preventing exit, and the ancient secretary whose name was still unknown to me, I suggested we would be wise to speak privately. "May we go into your office?"

"Very well. But I will not be fobbed off, sir. I demand an explanation."

"You shall hear all," I assured him.

The manager led the way up some stairs to a landing where a door was labelled Francis Gerard Prange. He took out a key, opened the door and switching on a light held the door wide permitting me to enter before him. The room was a typical office only made unusual by the great number of pictures both hanging on the walls and stacked against them on the floor. Dotted about in places that were obviously temporary were several sculptures and ornamental pots.

"Sit down, sir," said the manager indicating a chair in front of a great desk which was also overflowing with papers and artistic artefacts. He took his place behind it in what was obviously his customary seat. "Now, sir. Speak!" he commanded.

"I take it you are Mr Prange?" He nodded assent. "Then you must know that tonight the Chamber Music Society of Baker Street was to have a recital by Signor Salvato known as the Gloved Pianist."

"I've spent the day getting my staff to move all the exhibits from the room and set out the chairs for the recital," he said frostily.

"Well the evening commenced as planned right up to the entrance of Signor Salvato. He entered, struck a few chords on the piano and then dropped down dead."

"Dead?" he repeated with incredulity.

"Not only dead, Mr Prange, but murdered."

"Murdered? Murdered?" he repeated in bewilderment.

"Yes. I understand your amazement. The situation must be unique in the annals of crime. Signor Salvato met his end by means of poison entering his blood stream from cuts on his fingers." All the bluster had drained away from the man as I explained. "The man died in full view of the audience."

"But – the police must be called," he whispered.

"They have, sir. An ambulance was summoned, the dead man taken away. We currently await an inspector from Scotland Yard. You will, I am sure, now understand why people are being prevented from leaving the hall. If, as Mr Sherlock Holmes suspects, the murderer is someone actually present in the hall, they cannot possibly be allowed the opportunity to escape."

"Mr Sherlock Holmes, you say? Is he here in the gallery?"

"Indeed he is. The circumstances could not be more fortuitous. Mr Holmes was attending the recital as a member of the audience. Perhaps you know of Mr Holmes?"

"Indeed. And now of course, I realise who you are! You are his friend and biographer Dr Watson."

"I did introduce myself," I assured him.

"You did, you did, but I was so annoyed that although I heard your name I did not associate it with the Dr Watson of literary fame. I do apologise for swearing at you, Dr Watson, but I really could not get a sensible answer from those men at the door."

"Perfectly understandable, Mr Prange. For my part I feared you were a newspaper reporter attempting to force entrance."

"The newspapers!" he cried. "This will ruin me, doctor. Nobody will want to visit a gallery where a man has been murdered."

Privately I was not so sure of that. My feeling was more that the public, or a certain section of it, would be positively attracted to visit such a spot. "I think you may find that whilst some of your more refined clients may stay away, a lot of new faces will appear to inspect the exhibits in your galleries."

"I do not wish my galleries to be an attraction for the mere voyeur and thrill seeker, Dr Watson."

"Indeed no, but I have found in my experience that in any group of people there are always those who are open to new experience. People may come out of curiosity but they will have to look at your works of art even if they are doing it as a pretence to see the place where the lurid murder happened. Some of those people will like what they see and some will come back time and time again as you change your exhibitions, and some will buy a work of art."

"Humm," mused Prange, "perhaps you're right."

"In any case, whilst I can assure you that the papers will not hear of this affair from myself or Mr Holmes, there are two hundred people down there and they all have friends and neighbours. It is inevitable that they will return home and tomorrow tell of the strange evening they have endured. It is bound to end up in the papers and I regret nothing can prevent it."

Prange sighed. "I am afraid you're right, Doctor. But what is to be done tonight? What is Mr Holmes doing as we sit here."

"He is gathering clues and interviewing many of audience. When the police arrive they will, of course, make an official investigation. Mr Holmes is highly regarded by Scotland Yard and his analyses will be taken as the beginning of the operation. At the moment the members are resigned to waiting until there are developments of some sort but their patience is not infinite and the bolder members will start demanding to be allowed to leave. The police have powers to compulsorily detain them if required; Mr Holmes and I have not."

"Then what is to be done?"

"I have every hope that Mr Holmes will be able to find the murderer. Whether he can do this tonight is a moot point. At present the members are enjoying conversing with each other and occupying themselves looking at the pictures on the walls."

"Those are the remnants of the 8th Annual Exhibition of the Arts and Crafts Society which has just finished. That gallery was full of furniture, ceramics, glassware and all manner of household goods designed by members of that society. We cleared all those away to set out the seating. The items on the walls are mainly wallpaper and fabric designs and sketches of houses, gardens and plans."

This was the explanation for the rather peculiar pictures I had noted. Some seemed to comprise only of repetitious patterns which had puzzled me; now I realised they were wallpaper and fabric designs.

"Well it is fortunate there is something for them to see. Who knows, you may receive some sales as a result, Mr Prange."

"Thank you for your explanation, doctor, but I still do not see why I cannot enter my own gallery. After all, when the murder was committed I was up here in my office and I am seeking to enter, not flee, the hall."

"Very true, Mr Prange. I am sure you may enter your gallery should you wish to do so. I will, of course, have to ask Mr Holmes, in case it conflicts with his plans, but I am sure he will permit it. However, I must warn you that if you are known to the members they will undoubtedly accost you and seek to know what you propose to do."

"Me? I will not be able to tell them anything. Nothing at all."

"Of course not, but if they know you are the manager of the building you will be regarded as the person in charge and they will look to you for their salvation. The police, too, will require to speak with you. Have you a cogent reason for wishing to enter the hall?"

"Well, no, no, not really. I was just outraged at not being permitted to enter. Now you have explained all I am amply satisfied."

"If you were on your way home, Mr Prange, I advise you to do so. After all you could well have done so already. I presume you do not always work so late. You will have to speak to the police in the morning, of course. I will be here when they come and I will explain to them that you know the circumstances and that you were given leave to go by Mr Holmes and that you will be here in the morning at – what time, shall we say? Nine o'clock?"

"Yes, yes. I will do that. Perhaps things will be clearer by then and I will know whether I can open the gallery or not."

"May I have your home address in case Mr Holmes or the police wish to contact you there."

"Yes, yes, of course. My card," said he proffering it to me.

We left the office and returned to the ground floor where Mr Prange hurried away before he could be detained, saying that his caretaker would lock up at the end of the night as usual. I returned to find Holmes as I had left him, pondering the suspects on the list I had drawn up.

"We have heard Mr Redvers-Gordon and Mr Morello explain their reasons for visiting the piano prior to the concert starting. Perhaps those reasons were not as innocent as they claim? We also know that a deadly South American poison was administered – a poison that Mr Redvers-Gordon freely admits he brought into this country. He then claims to have lost track of it. Miss Norman, who carried on an illicit *affaire* with Mr Redvers-Gordon, had ample opportunity to abstract the phial of poison on one of her many visits to Mr Redvers-Gordon's house. Miss Norman likes to give the impression she is a self-centred shallow lady who knows nothing apart from her world of the theatre. A world of frivolity and vanity. But the fact that she is able to string along one man after another shows she is cunning and deceitful. Men like the pathetic Mr Morello have their emotions twisted by her so they become desperate. Possibly desperate enough to kill. And then we have Mr Shawcross who is an astute business man manufacturing under licence the latest invention – a safety razor blade. An ironic object seeing it brought the opposite to safety to poor Mr Salvato, the Gloved Pianist. Does all this simply mean *cherchez la femme*, Watson?"

"You think Miss Norman the murderer? Certainly she is ruthless in the matter of *beaux* but surely she would not stoop to murder?" I protested.

"Who knows to what ends a woman scorned will go?"

"You think she took revenge on Salvato over some lover's quarrel?"

"We have only her word that she left him. It is perfectly possible that in fact he threw her over and, as a result, she thirsted for revenge. As she admitted to us, she is not a lady who submits herself to any man's beck and call."

"Yes and she also said that she parted not without some regrets. As you say, perhaps it was Salvato who threw her out and not the other way. And she could have got the blades from her current lover Shawcross. That would be very neat, Holmes, poison from one ex-*beau*, blades from another to gain revenge on a third."

"We must also face the possibility that none of these persons is guilty. Who was that you went to see at the door?"

"Mr Prange the manager of the establishment."

"Indeed? Where is he now?"

"I allowed him to go home. He was in his office until he came down and was refused admittance. That was the fuss he was making that I went to sort out. This is his card with his home address and he has promised to be here by nine in the morning should you or the police wish to speak to him. He was in his office throughout and did not know anything about the murder until I informed him. I do not think he is in any way suspicious. It is incredible that he should instigate a public murder on his own premises. He is very afraid that the notoriety will cause him to lose business."

"Whenever you have eliminated the impossible, whatever remains, no matter how improbable, must be the truth."

"Yes, Holmes," I agreed meekly. He had said that very thing many times before.

"Come, Watson, we must speak to all these people out there who are totally innocent and unnecessarily detained."

We returned to the hall where Holmes found Porter the chairman doing his best to reassure several members who were agitating to leave for home.

"Ah, here is Mr Holmes, perhaps he can tell us something further."

"Mr Chairman, please ask everyone to return to their seats so that I can address the audience," said Holmes briskly.

His commanding manner ensured that the muttered protests ceased and the disputatious members willingly obeyed him as Porter mounted the dais and banged his gavel loudly several times to silence the chattering throng.

"Ladies and Gentlemen please return to your places, Mr Sherlock Holmes wishes to speak to you all."

I have always thought Holmes would have made a superb actor. I have witnessed many examples of his skill with make-up and disguise and an almost protean ability to transform his figure and voice. His spare frame conceals a commanding presence and whilst rarely being in the position of an orator his natural authority demands attention. Silence fell as he mounted the dais.

"Ladies and gentlemen thank you for your patience. You have been most understanding under the most harrowing circumstances. We expect the police to arrive at any moment to take charge of the proceedings but I feel I may be able to assist them by the preliminary enquiries I have been making. That Signor Salvato met his unfortunate end by murder there is not a shadow of doubt. I also suspect that the perpetrator of this heinous crime is still with us in the hall."

This statement caused much consternation as people looked around at their neighbours fearing they could be seated next to the villain. I wondered if Holmes were wise to make such an assertion. Surely it could only result in alerting the murderer.

Lord Challis spoke up. "Do you know the identity of this evil man, Mr Holmes?"

"You say man, Lord Challis, but there are many ladies in this room."

"Surely you do not accuse a lady of this vile deed?" protested Lord Challis amidst the dismay and horror that Holmes's statement provoked.

"As yet I accuse nobody, my lord, but this death was caused not by brute strength, attacking with some weapon, but very simply by a method that is well within the capabilities of any female. It takes no more than simple cunning to dip a few razor blades in poison and place them in a position where the victim inadvertently cuts himself."

"Well I'm not having any of these new-fangled blades in my house!" called out some wag thereby causing a ripple of nervous laughter.

"You may call them new-fangled now, but by the end of the year all you fellows will be using them," retorted Hudson Shawcross.

"I am sure you are right, Mr Shawcross," replied Holmes, "but the fact remains that tonight in this hall – you seem to be the only one who knows anything about such a thing. I now ask you to humour me in this – it is important. Will all the gentlemen who are members of this society raise their left hand?"

I could not imagine the purpose of this but Holmes never did anything without a reason so as a member himself he raised his hand along with most of the gentlemen in the room.

"Thank you," continued Holmes. "Now would the gentlemen who are not members but visitors and guests please raise their right hand." Far fewer men's hands, including my own, rose in the air.

"Thank you. You have been most co-operative." He turned to the chairman who was standing on the floor by the side of the dais. "Mr Porter you have been most helpful in dealing with this turbulent evening. I do wonder, however, why you pass yourself off as an Englishman when you are in fact Italian. You have mastered the English language excellently yet there are lapses when you are agitated. Also you use Italian expressions when an Englishman would not. A true born Englishman would normally say 'open air' not '*al fresco*'. You referred to an ambulanza rather than an ambulance and you used the Italian form Parigi for the city we call Paris and so on. The town called Folkestone was obviously unfamiliar to you as you pronounced the name in an incorrect manner."

The silence that descended on the audience was profound. Porter obviously felt a response was called for.

"So I am not a true-born Englishman. I may have suffered in the lottery of life by not being born an Englishman but, as far as I am aware, it is not yet a crime to be a foreigner to these shores."

"No," agreed Holmes, "your nationality is not a crime but in this country murder is, even if in your homeland such a thing is treated more casually."

"Curse you, Holmes! You'll never take me alive!" cried Porter as he ran for the emergency exit thrusting the guards out of the way and crashing the doors open as he dashed outside.

"After him, Watson!" I needed no urging from Holmes, being already through the door and on the villain's tail. I found myself in a passage not much more than a yard wide and saw my quarry silhouetted at the end where he was outlined against the lights of the street lamps in Bond Street. He dashed out of my sight as he ran straight out and tried to cross Bond Street. As I gained the main road I saw him run into the path of a motor car that was just pulling up outside the entrance to the Galleries. A Pierce Arrow tonneau. The chauffeur didn't have a chance and the car ploughed into Porter.

* * *

It was good to be back home in our rooms at 221b Baker Street after such a tumultuous evening. The police, in the guise of our old friend Lestrade and a number of constables, had arrived and we had thus been detained further while Holmes gave statements and explanations.

"Shall we have a nightcap, Watson? I feel too invigorated to seek my bed as yet."

"Are you going to tell me how you deduced the murderer?" I asked pouring our drinks. "I do not know when Porter could have placed the blades on the keyboard."

"He had ample time to place the razor blades after introducing Miss Norman at the very beginning of the evening. You will recall that Miss Norman and Mr Shawcross stepped up on to the dais thus completely hiding Porter for a full half minute while Miss Norman boosted her forthcoming musical comedy. I am afraid, Watson, that you put rather a red herring in our way by suggesting that the tattoo on the wrist of Signor Salvato the Gloved Pianist was a love token. When our worthy chairman delighted us during the concert with his interminable folk songs which he rendered in such an overblown theatrical manner, he exposed his left wrist. I observed his wrist carried the same tattoo. This I confirmed when he exposed it again during my request for the gentlemen members to raise their left hands."

"So that's why you made the appeal? I could not see the point of the request as, if it were important, any man could easily lie by refraining from raising his hand."

"An expedient to get another look at Porter's tattoo to confirm my theory. How else could I have achieved that without raising his suspicion?"

"But what is the significance of the tattoos?" asked I in puzzlement.

"The initials CN stand not for the delightful Miss Celia Norman, as you suggested, but for the Italian words *Cosa Nostra*. A secret society perhaps better known as the mafia. Salvato was obviously a member of the brotherhood – Miss Norman said she met his brothers in Sicily, the home of the *Cosa Nostra*. Salvato is an old Sicilian family name. Salvato wore white gloves so that the tattoo would not be revealed when he played the piano. The chairman was what is known in American gangster circles as a 'hitman'. He was sent by his masters to assassinate Salvato who had obviously transgressed in some way."

"Porter made a very convincing Englishman, Holmes, I'll give him that."

"Yes, but perhaps my suspicions should have been aroused earlier as I noted the soubriquet he had chosen for himself. Walter Porter is the name of an English composer of the early 17th century, a pupil of Monteverdi, composer of many madrigals. I suspect he saw the name on a piece of music and thought it sounded typically English. He thought boasting that he was from Whitechapel added to the verisimilitude. No Englishman would flaunt the fact he lived in Whitechapel."

"He was right that we would never take him alive. He did not have a chance when that car ran into him."

"As an author, Watson, no doubt you will make much of the irony that the motor car belonged to Mr Hudson Shawcross who had ordered his chauffeur to collect him at ten o'clock. Tonight has been unique in my long experience – two deaths by means that would have been impossible just a few years ago. Safety razor blades and a motor car."

"Modern times, Holmes."

"Yes, Watson.  Modern methods but the same age-old lusts and passions."

"The concert proved more interesting than you expected."

"Indeed.  But I trust you will not compel me to attend any further events of the Baker Street Chamber Music Society. My musical tastes are really rather more elevated."

"No, Holmes.  Neither will I repeat my error.  Next Christmas it will be back to your favourite tobacco."

SHERLOCK HOLMES
and the Singular Adventure
of

THE GLOVED PIANIST


THE PLAY

## AUTHOR'S NOTE

The first part of the story you have just read is a reworking of a pastiche called *The Singular Adventure of the Vanishing Nobleman* which appeared in the first edition of my collection *The Singular Adventures of Mr Sherlock Holmes* (2003). This tale was dropped from the second more successful enlarged edition (2006) which contained three additional new stories. These versions now being out of print, a third edition of this book by Vesper Hawk Publishing is now available (2010).

The play version of *The Singular Adventure of the Gloved Pianist* was created in the form of the popular "Murder Mystery" evenings and had its first performance on 9th February 2008 at a village in Kent. I did not wish the play to be something merely watched in a conventional manner so the *mise-en-scene* is designed to embrace, include and make the audience part of the action. It is also to be regarded as a fun evening with the audience in period costumes entering into the spirit of the occasion and, whilst not intended as a lampoon or spoof, the work, as such is essentially amusing and light-hearted and contains puns and jokes.

The premiere was graced by a small party of Sherlockians from The Sherlock Holmes Society of London who travelled down to the country to join the locals. A review, giving an impression of how the event was seen by the audience, subsequently appeared in the Sherlock Holmes Journal and this is reproduced here by kind permission of the editor.

## THE SINGULAR ADVENTURE
## OF THE
## GLOVED PIANIST
### Reviewed by JONATHAN McCAFFERTY

SMARDEN IN KENT would be recognised by lovers of Agatha Christie films, for the village provides a home for Miss Marple (Angela Lansbury) in *The Mirror Crack'd*. One envies Miss Marple, for Smarden has many awards as the prettiest village in Kent. Good Queen Bess recognised Smarden's merits through the grant of a charter.

One night in February 2008 a small party of Sherlockians joined the village folk in the modern-day Charter Hall for the debut of *The Singular Adventure of the Gloved Pianist,* specially devised for the hall by Alan Stockwell. The year was 1905; we were transported to a concert hall in Baker Street. Mr Tony Lush, the chairman for this evening's gathering of the Baker Street Chamber Music Society, announced that we were graced by the presence of Miss Celia Norman, who would shortly be starring in *The Beggar Princess* on the West End stage. Miss Norman (Lea Randolph), a ravishing beauty, rose to acknowledge our applause. The chairman continued by telling us that the musical programme consisted of a performance by "The Aspidistra Quartet", four local youngsters who played Bach arrangements for wind instruments, with a guest appearance by Guido Salvato, the famous gloved pianist. I noted that one music lover on my table seemed to have entered a dream-like state and had the irritating habit of wafting his hands in time with the music. Our chairman gave a rendition of that old monologue "The Green Eye of the Yellow God". There was little opportunity to consider the misadventures of Mad Carew before the great Guido Salvato, played with great aplomb by Peter Gibbs, took the stage. His dainty cotton evening gloves were prominent. The gloved hands descended to the piano keyboard with a resounding fortissimo. Moments later he tumbled from his piano stool and lay prone upon the floor!

A call for medical assistance summoned Doctor Watson, played as deferential by the slight, moustachioed figure of Mike Twort. Only a cursory examination was required before the fateful diagnosis: "He's dead." The chairman asked that an ambulance be called. Dr Watson exclaimed that the gloved pianist's hands were covered with blood. The stentorian admonition: "Don't touch the keyboard!" brought our Society's very own Auberon Redfearn to the stage as a very elegant, gentlemanly Sherlock Holmes, with a quiet but compelling authority and intense, intelligent observation. Having instructed that no one should leave the hall, the master detective engaged in a minute examination of the dear departed and further clues were provided – not only had the gloves been slashed but a cryptic tattoo was revealed on the dead man's wrist. Further investigation showed that razor blades impregnated with curare, a fatal poison of South American origin, had been sandwiched between the piano keys. These had promptly caused the asphyxiation of Guido Salvato. Who was responsible for this dreadful deed? Where had these new fangled razor blades been obtained? And how on earth could deadly curare have surfaced in the metropolis?

The remaining part of the first Act furnished the audience with plentiful clues and just as many red-herrings. Mr Holmes informed us that disposable safety razors were an American product newly imported into England. Mr Hudson Shawcross, a business magnate (played by Richard Vernon with a no-nonsense robustness), stepped forward and stated that he was the sole importer. In flat Yorkshire vowels Mr Shawcross agreed that he had distributed a limited number of prototypes prior to general sale. One of the wind quartet observed that the keyboard had nothing harmful before the audience arrived. Dr Watson pointed to a distinguished looking gent, spotted as coming on stage immediately before the recital – the well-known pianist and composer Aubrey Morrello (played by Reyner Missing). Ablaze with professional jealousy, Mr Morrello denounced the late Salvato as an "idle useless fellow", his gloves a mere gimmick, who had enjoyed great success while Morrello, despite achieving academic honours, had not tasted the worldly joys of financial success. Morrello insisted that he was innocent and challenged Holmes to prove otherwise. One did not have to look far for the source of the curare: a fellow wearing a pith helmet was near at hand. This was the fearless man of action Edmund Redvers-Gordon (played by Hilary Millen). The great explorer declared that a sudden withdrawal of funds by his patron had caused delay to a planned exploration of darkest Africa. The moneys were now diverted to music and the arts and Mr Redvers-Gordon had turned up this evening to see what the cash had purchased. He was familiar with curare from Amazon journeys; it was fatal if it touched an open wound. Indeed, until recently the explorer had a sample phial amongst a vast collection in his library. Its current whereabouts were unknown. Happily Mr Redvers-Gordon had found the means of replacing the missing funds and intended to sail for Africa the next day. His reason for attending the concert was to say a fond farewell to a certain lady who was now on the arm of Mr Shawcross, the Yorkshire magnate. All heads turned to see Miss Celia Norman totter at the revelation. Recovering her composure, Miss Norman revealed that she provided the links between all the protagonists, for each had enjoyed her embraces. First came Redvers-Gordon (dismissed as "boring"), then Salvato (but the gloved pianist departed for Italy), so she found herself in the arms of Aubrey Morrello, (too poor to sustain her affections). All these were mere peccadilloes, declared Miss Norman; at last she had found true love in the plutocratic Hudson Shawcross.

So we came to our dinner interval with four suspects to consider. Members of the cast chatted amiably with the audience. I noted that Mr Shawcross was particularly keen to name somebody else as the culprit. There was no unanimity of verdict at our table for any one of these doubtful characters could have done the dreadful deed. All was revealed by Sherlock Holmes in a tour de force of deductive powers which composed a brief second Act.

Thus ended a most enjoyable evening; a Sherlockian who-done-it with dinner. The author, Alan Stockwell, is no stranger to Holmesian pastiche and his published work has recently been reprinted for a wider readership amongst a selection in *Sherlock Holmes: The Game's Afoot* (edited by David Stuart Davies, Wordsworth editions). In an excellent piece of dinner theatre Mr Stockwell has provided a most successful divertissement, with strong period characterisation and intriguing drama. The format was such that with a little effort (and the author's consent) it may be readily staged by any small company.

It would be most unfair of this reviewer to disclose the *denouement,* as with any luck the play may be put on again near you.

# SHERLOCK HOLMES MYSTERY EVENING
## "The Singular Adventure of the Gloved Pianist"

## CONCEPT

The concept is that all the people attending the Mystery Evening are members of a music club "The Baker Street Chamber Music Society" enjoying a concert in London in the year 1905. Therefore some members will be acquainted with others whilst some will not. During the evening there is a supper interval. Prizes may be given for the best period costumes. A raffle can be held with appropriate thematic prizes.

The arrangement of the audience may be theatre-style facing a stage, in which case the members of the audience will take refreshments in another room during the interval and then return to the theatre for the dénouement. A preferable arrangement is to have the room arranged cabaret-style with a raised dais, platform, rostrum or podium about 15" high for the performers. The hall may be decorated in keeping with the period and if, as they should, all the people come in costume there is much pleasure from mixing and mingling during the course of the evening. Members may thus drink at their tables throughout and later take supper *in situ*. The following script is written with this arrangement in mind.

Most of the dialogue is scripted and therefore acted as in a play but the "play" takes place in and amongst the audience and they are actually participants in the drama. The actors enacting the roles must be capable of improvising around their scripted parts if it should be necessary. Such opportunities are tightly controlled if the script is rigidly adhered to. The play, in both action and dialogue, offers clues which are intended to lead the observer to several different people so that, during the course of the evening, the emphasis on the suspects changes as more information is revealed. Before the dénouement by Holmes the audience is given the opportunity to vote for their particular suspect.

The progress of the evening is

- STRAIGHT CONCERT ITEMS. Preferably several short light pieces by a string quartet but this will depend on the musical resources available. However, it is essential that the piano is not used by anyone other than Signor Salvato.
- SOLO BY THE CHAIRMAN. This may be a song accompanied by a guitar or some other instrument but not the piano, or a recitation of the period eg *The Green Eye of the Little Yellow God.* The Chairman's solo can follow the musical items or can be placed during them. This concert part of the programme should last about twenty minutes although if the performers are of high standard the audience may well like it a little longer.
- MURDER OF THE GLOVED PIANIST thus bringing the concert to an interrupted end.
- INVESTIGATION BY HOLMES & WATSON who interview the suspects.
- BREAK FOR SUPPER enabling the audience to discuss and talk to the suspects, Holmes and Watson.
- PRIZE WINNING COSTUMES and RAFFLE (optional)
- CONCLUSION when HOLMES sums up the position, audience "votes" and the murderer is revealed.

# SHERLOCK HOLMES MYSTERY EVENING
## "The Singular Adventure of the Gloved Pianist"

## CAST

SHERLOCK HOLMES
DR WATSON
CHAIRMAN of the Baker Street Chamber Music Society
HUDSON SHAWCROSS a wealthy steel magnate
CELIA NORMAN a flighty West End musical comedy star
EDMUND REDVERS-GORDON a dour explorer
AUBREY MORELLO an excitable English musician
GUIDO SALVATO the Gloved Pianist (a non-speaking rôle)
MUSICAL ENSEMBLE (the leader has a few lines)
SPECTATOR 1 (if no actor is available a genuine member of the audience may on arrival be given a card with the lines and instructed to read them out when required)
NEWCOMER (if no actor is available a genuine member of the audience may on arrival be given a card with the lines and instructed to read them out when required)

HOLMES, WATSON, SHAWCROSS & NORMAN, REDVERS-GORDON, MORELLO, SPECTATOR 1, are all seated dispersed amongst the audience.

**THE SCENE** is a concert given for members of the Chamber Music Society of Baker Street. The year is 1905. The CHAIRMAN is in charge of the proceedings, welcoming the members, introducing the items etc. The concert is given by:

    a) A MUSICAL ENSEMBLE
    b) THE GLOVED PIANIST

    and the CHAIRMAN also gives a solo during the proceedings.

# PART ONE

As the members come in and seat themselves the CHAIRMAN is fluttering around greeting them.

EDMUND REDVERS-GORDON stops as he passes the piano and peers intently about it before taking his seat.

As the seats fill AUBREY MORELLO wanders up to the piano and flicks through the music on the stand and returns to his seat.

Just before the start of the concert HUDSON SHAWCROSS, with CELIA NORMAN on his arm, comes in with the CHAIRMAN bowing and scraping and ushering them to their seats in the front row. Their seats are directly in front of the piano. The Chairman steps on to the podium

**CHAIRMAN:**  Your attention please, everybody!  We are about to start the concert but first – ladies and gentlemen, we are very honoured to have with us this evening as our guest of honour, the famous star of the West End stage Miss Celia Norman!

NORMAN and SHAWCROSS step up on to the dais. NORMAN flings out her arms and speaks.  During this speech NORMAN and SHAWCROSS are standing facing the audience and the CHAIRMAN is behind them.

**NORMAN:**  Good evening everyone!  I'm so thrilled to be asked to come here tonight to your little musical soirée. After bringing delight to so many of you it is lovely for me to be able to sit and listen to other people providing the music.  As many of you will know I am shortly to start rehearsals for my new show *The Beggar Princess* which will open next month at Daly's Theatre. It's a delightful musical comedy written by that wonderful composer Lionel Monckton. I play a poor beggar girl who turns out to be a princess. There are some beautiful new songs in it. I do hope to see you all there.

**The pair step down and seat themselves.**

**CHAIRMAN:** It is a great honour to welcome such an illustrious adornment of the West End stage to our humble musical entertainment. And you too, sir, are most welcome. (*bows*) Well we are now ready to commence the concert. Later on we have a very famous star attraction – The Gloved Pianist. As you know, this gentleman hails from Italy and has captured the imagination of audiences all over the continent with his virtuoso playing whilst wearing white gloves. It is a great capture for us to have him with us tonight. But first please welcome our musical ensemble for this evening – the Aspidistra Trio! **(or whatever the ensemble is called)**

**The musicians file in and take their places at their instruments. They do not use the piano.**

**Now follows a straight programme of musical entertainment. This may be as popular or highbrow as suits your audience, but it must be authentic to the year 1905. Perhaps a few musical pieces interspersed with ballads of the time.**

**During the course of the concert the CHAIRMAN sings a song (if he is not a singer a dramatic recitation such as *"The Green Eye of the Little Yellow God"* may be substituted) during which he stretches an arm so that**

his left wrist shows.

After the planned programme has been gone through (about 20 mins) the CHAIRMAN speaks.

**CHAIRMAN:**  And now we come to the star of the evening – a musician of extraordinary talent who has set all of Europe aflame.  I first saw this talented pianist at an al fresco[2] concert in Folk-es-ton[3].  Please welcome Signor Guido Salvato – the Gloved Pianist!

Enter THE GLOVED PIANIST who seats himself at the piano.  He starts to play but immediately leaps to his feet shouting in agony, thrusts his hands into his armpits and falls to the ground.  The CHAIRMAN rushes up and stoops over the crumpled body on the floor.  He stands and addresses the audience.

**CHAIRMAN:**  I think he has collapsed.  I am very sorry ladies and gentlemen but Signor Salvato seems to have been taken ill.  Is there a doctor in the house?

**WATSON:**(*rising*)  I'm a Doctor, John H Watson, late Indian Army.

**CHAIRMAN:**  Oh, sir, if you would be so good as to come forth.

Dr WATSON comes to the front and examines the prone PIANIST whilst the CHAIRMAN hovers anxiously. WATSON soon stands.

**WATSON:**  He's dead.

**CHAIRMAN:**  Dead?  How can this be?

**WATSON:**   Probably a heart attack – I have no medical equipment with me, I cannot examine him properly. (*looking down*)  Good God!

**CHAIRMAN:**   What is it?

**WATSON:**   Look at his hands!  (*He lifts a wrist - the gloves are covered in blood*)  They are covered in blood!  What has happened?

Bewildered, Watson stares about then reaches out to the piano keyboard.

**HOLMES:**   (*rising in the audience*) Watson!  Don't touch the keyboard!

**CHAIRMAN:**   What is this?  I do not understand!

**HOLMES:**   (*coming forward*)  I am Sherlock Holmes the famous detective.  I must examine this man.  Touch nothing!  (*Holmes comes to the front and takes charge*)  Nobody must leave this hall.  You, sir, station one of your staff at every exit.  Go on, man, don't just stand staring!

**CHAIRMAN:**   Yes, yes, of course. (*muttering*) Mamma Mia![4] (*He hurries out*)

**HOLMES:**   (*to the musicians*)  Please play something whilst I examine this man.

The musicians play a tune.  When the music stops HOLMES rises.

**HOLMES:**   Watson, when you examined the man's hands did you notice a tattoo on the inside of the wrist?

**WATSON:**   I did but I did not remark it.

**HOLMES:**   Take a close look.

   WATSON examines man's wrist.

**WATSON:**   It seems to be a device with the letters C and N.

**HOLMES:**   (*holding out a slashed white glove covered in blood*) And what do you make of that Watson?

**WATSON:**   Good heavens, Holmes, the fellow's gloves are cut to ribbons. What does this mean?

**HOLMES:**   It means that this innocent looking musical instrument is a deadly weapon. Stand clear, Watson.

   HOLMES with tweezers in one hand, handkerchief in the other, goes along the keyboard and extracts razor blades from between the keys with the tweezers, holding each one aloft, and lays them on the handkerchief.

**WATSON:**   What are they Holmes? They look like tiny knives. Diabolical!

**HOLMES:**   I fancy these are the new invention of the American Mr King Camp Gillette.

**WATSON:**   New invention?

**HOLMES:**   A new type of razor to enable gentlemen to shave in safety.

**WATSON:**   I've never heard of such a thing.

**SHAWCROSS:** *(rising)* If I may make so bold as to interrupt you, Mr Holmes. You are correct.  Indeed they are disposable razor blades.  I have heard of your reputation and we are indeed fortunate to have you here at the very time the murder was committed.

**HOLMES:**   You say 'murder', sir?

**SHAWCROSS:**   Well, yes.  It would seem to be that someone has chosen this bizarre method to kill the gloved pianist.

**HOLMES:**   One might see that a malicious person, a jealous rival, perhaps, may wish to damage a musician's hands in this manner but why do you say murder?

**SHAWCROSS:**   The man's dead, isn't he?

**HOLMES:**   True, but perhaps the shock of slashing his fingers caused a heart attack.

**SHAWCROSS:**   Then the malicious person you speak of has caused more damage than he intended.

**HOLMES:**   You are correct. It is certainly murder. *(he smells the blades in his hand)*  These blades have been dipped into a deadly poison – a type of  curare.  A poison in which the Amazonian Indians dip their arrows before putting them in their blowpipes.  This poison is so deadly that the tiniest amount on an open wound is instant death. The pianist had no chance – as soon as his fingers were cut the poison entered his system and stopped his breath. The man died from asphyxia.  It seems significant that you immediately assumed the death was murder. Tell me about these blades, sir, you seem to know about them.

WATSON takes out his pocketbook and starts making notes.

**SHAWCROSS:**  I should do – I manufacture them.

**HOLMES:**  Indeed?

**SHAWCROSS:**  My name is Hudson Shawcross.

**WATSON:**  The famous steel magnate?

**SHAWCROSS:**  The same.

**WATSON:**  I hear all the ladies are attracted to you.

**SHAWCROSS:**  That is because I am a magnate.

**HOLMES:**  You realise, sir, that by admitting to being a maker of these things you are putting yourself under great suspicion.

**SHAWCROSS:**  Nonsense, sir! Mr King Camp Gillette invented this system to ease gentlemen's shaving. Blades came into use in the USA last year and now they have come to Britain. As you will know, whatever America does first we Britons follow. I have Mr Gillette's licence to manufacture his product here. So it's no more of the old cut-throat razor – we chaps can now use these disposable blades in a safety holder that bends the flexible blade to the right angle and bob's your uncle. They are not yet on sale in this country, but prototypes have been widely distributed. And any fellow who has travelled to America could have brought some back with him. So no more expensive trips to the barber and no more the hazard of nicking your own face.

**HOLMES:**  So these things will be on general sale?

**SHAWCROSS:**  Very shortly, sir; in packets of five blades.  The holders are available separately.  I don't have the rights for making those.

**HOLMES:**  Thank you, Mr Shawcross for your explanation.  We are much in your debt.  It is clear that anyone in the hall could have used this dastardly method of murder.

    The CHAIRMAN re-enters

**CHAIRMAN:**  I have guards posted at every door, Mr Holmes. They all know what to do if anyone tries to leave the building. I have also summoned an ambulanza[5] which will be here in a very short time.

**HOLMES:**  Excellent, you have done well.

**MUSICIAN:**  May I speak, sir?

**HOLMES:**  Of course.

**MUSICIAN:**  I can definitely say that those things were not on the piano keyboard before the audience entered the hall.

**HOLMES:**  You are sure of that?

**MUSICIAN:**  Most definitely.  We were rehearsing right up to the time the doors were opened to permit the entrance of the audience.  Even as the first arrivals were seating themselves I was hastily putting the bandstand in order and the last thing I did was to check the keyboard and give it a final dusting.  To have it perfect for our star guest.  I could not have missed seeing several metal blades.

**HOLMES:**   That is most significant.  This means that the murderer must have placed the razor blades between the keys between the time of the first arrivals and the beginning of the concert.  (*to audience*)  Did anyone see any person approach the piano prior to the start of the concert?

**[NOTE:**  This point will have to be taken ad lib depending on the response.  There are three possibilities:
a)  EDMUND REDVERS-GORDON was seen by somebody
b)  AUBREY MORELLO was seen by somebody
c)  Nobody admits to seeing anybody.
If there is no response at all WATSON will have to say he saw "that gentleman approach the piano and do some fiddling with the sheets of music on the stand" and indicate MORELLO.  Holmes then proceeds as follows.
If REDVERS-GORDON is indicated by somebody then WATSON will have to say "I also saw that gentleman" and indicate MORELLO.  But however it is contrived, MORELLO must be the next to be interviewed.]

**HOLMES:**   May I ask your name sir?

**MORELLO:**   (*standing*)  My name is Aubrey Morello.  It may be known to some of the members here as I am a pianist and composer.

**CHAIRMAN:**   Mr Morello is one of our most distinguished members, Mr Holmes, he often performs in Parigi[6] where his works are well known.

**HOLMES:**   Neither the name or the face are known to me.  Were you to play for us tonight?

**MORELLO:**   Not tonight.  The field was clear for that so-called pianist.

**HOLMES:**   In that case, Mr Morello, perhaps you would tell us why you approached the piano when you are here, not as a performer, but a mere member of the audience?

**MORELLO:**   There is no mystery, sir.  I went to examine the programme to be played by that charlatan the so called Gloved Pianist.

**HOLMES:**   Were you not content to wait like the rest of us, to see what delights were in store?

**MORELLO:**   I wanted to be sure he was not intending to play any of my works.

**HOLMES:**   I see.  You did not want him to do that?

**MORELLO:**   Certainly not!  The man is nothing but a low class music hall performer masquerading as a classical pianist.

**HOLMES:**   I take it from the vehemence of your reply that you did not like the man.

**MORELLO:**   I hated him!  I have hated Salvato since we were fellow students at the Paris Conservatoire.

**HOLMES:**   What is the reason for this hatred?

**MORELLO:**   The reason is simple, Mr Holmes.  He was a gross, idle, useless fellow and a deplorable musician as a student and he is still the same now.  When he was a student Salvato scraped by doing the minimum of work, just avoiding being thrown out on his ear. Just because he was Italian he was favoured by the professors most of whom were Italian or French.  Whereas because I was an Englishman they never considered my talents.  The musical snobs do not think the English are musical.

**HOLMES:**  Morello does not appear to be an English name?

**MORELLO:**  It is a stage name.

**SHAWCROSS:**  Why choose to be named after a cherry?

**MORELLO:**  My true name is Morrell.  I added the O to give the impression I was Italian.  The English musical snobs don't think the English are musical either.  Salvato never even graduated yet somehow he has managed to persuade people he is a star pianist by means of this stupid gimmick of playing the piano with white gloves on.  Whereas I who graduated with the highest honours, won the Mozart prize for composition, a distinction in conducting, am compelled to a hand to mouth existence.

**HOLMES:**  But the chairman told us you have a distinguished career in Paris.  How can you now tell us you live in penury?

**MORELLO:**  Well perhaps I exaggerate when I say that, but my means are modest and whilst my compositions are highly regarded there is little money in original work.  I am very prolific and I have written many pieces that still wait for their first performance.  Unfortunately music lovers prefer to hear the music they know so we have endless recitals of Chopin and Beethoven while new work such as mine languishes unplayed.

**HOLMES:**  I see.  Well you have made your position very clear, Mr Morello.  However, you have placed yourself in a position of deep suspicion.  How do we know you did not take the opportunity to rid yourself of this man you so hated by placing razor blades between the keys? An act easily and swiftly done while you purported to riffle through the music book?

**MORELLO:** Though I wished the blaggard dead, I was not the hand that did the deed. Where would I obtain a deadly poison known only to the Amazon Indians?

**HOLMES:** In matters of this nature we cannot simply take your word, sir.

**MORELLO:** Of course not, sir. But if I wanted to kill the man would I not just shoot him? Or bludgeon him to death on a dark night? Would I contrive this bizarre public death for a man I hate? But if I am the murderer it is for you to prove my guilt not for me to prove my innocence.

**HOLMES:** I am well versed in the law of the land, sir. You may sit down. No doubt I shall need to question you further.

Two ambulance men enter with a stretcher to remove the corpse.

**CHAIRMAN:** Mr Holmes, is it in order for these men to remove the body?

**HOLMES:** Certainly, it can tell us nothing more. Take it straight to the morgue.

[**NOTE 1:** If there are not sufficient personnel the body can remain until the interval then surreptitiously leave via a judiciously placed screen and the two previous lines of dialogue omitted.]

**[NOTE 2:** If REDVERS-GORDON has previously been named, HOLMES now interviews him. If not he says (to the audience) "Now, ladies and gentlemen, I must ask you to think hard and carefully. Did you see anyone else near the piano prior to the start of the concert?"

Again this must be played ad lib. Perhaps SHAWCROSS and NORMAN may be suggested as their seats are near the piano but they must not be considered as they did not actually approach the piano. If there is no indication of REDVERS-GORDON then HOLMES himself can proceed on the following lines.**]**

**HOLMES:** I was seated over there and since taking my seat I observed two people approach the piano. Most people see but do not observe. I have trained my faculties so that I not only see but observe as well. The two people are Mr Morello, from whom we have just heard, the other person is – you, sir. (*points at Redvers-Gordon*) Would you do me the honour of coming forward?

**REDVERS-G:** (*rising and coming forward*) I have heard of your reputation, Mr Holmes. I should have known I could not escape your eagle eye.

**WATSON:** I believe I recognise you, sir. Are you not Edmund Redvers-Gordon the well-known explorer?

**REDVERS-G:** I am indeed, Dr Watson.

**WATSON:** I understood from the newspapers that you had recently left for Darkest Africa.

**REDVERS-G:** Indeed I should have been arriving in Matabeleland as we speak but just before my departure I heard that my source of funding had been abruptly withdrawn. I was all ready to leave when I had a message to say that the bankers' draft I was expecting would not be sent.  Without the funds I could not contemplate leaving. I am trying to raise money elsewhere.  My expedition is now pending but if I do not get money from somewhere the thing will shortly fall apart.

**WATSON:**  How unfortunate.  It seems most unkind and unorthodox to leave you in the lurch like that at the last minute.

**REDVERS-G:**  You put it most politely, sir.  I regret my reaction was far more intemperate.

**HOLMES:**  Do you mind disclosing the source of your funding and why it was so precipitately withdrawn?

**REDVERS-G:**  It's no secret, Mr Holmes.  It has been in the papers.  The Andrew Carnegie Foundation suddenly changed its policy.  It decided to increase its work with arts and music.  Apparently they think it more important to support a well-established culture well able to look after itself rather than help me explore the unknown recesses of the Dark Continent.  Hence this music society is able to afford to engage a star of the calibre of the Gloved Pianist.

**HOLMES:**  I see.  So are you a member of this society?

**REDVERS-G:**  No sir.  Music does not have particular charms for me.  I came as the guest of my friend here specifically to see – to see – the sort of thing that the Carnegie Foundation is supporting.  I feel very keenly the withdrawal of support from my expedition.

**HOLMES:**  Have you ever been to South America, Mr Redvers-Gordon?

**REDVERS-G:**  Yes, Mr Holmes.  I have spent some time in that continent.

**HOLMES:**  Perhaps you are familiar with the Amazon region?

**REDVERS-G:**  I am, and my discoveries there have led to increased knowledge of the area.  I venture to suggest that much of what you may know of the region is as a result of my endeavours.

**HOLMES:**  Does the term "velvet leaf" mean anything to you?

**REDVERS-G:**  It does.

**HOLMES:**  Perhaps you would explain it to us?

**REDVERS-G:**  Velvet leaf is a term the Witoto tribe of the Amazon forest use to describe a poisonous concoction.

**HOLMES:**  Do you wish to elaborate?

**REDVERS-G:**  It is a deadly poison made from the bark of *strychnos toxifera* mixed with *chrondrodendron tomentosum* to form a curare made even more virulent by the incorporation of toad and snake venom.  The Witoto boil this mess for two days.  The result is the most insidious poison known to man.  It is harmless if ingested by swallowing but if it enters the blood stream via an open gash or wound – death is instantaneous.  The Witoto dip their arrow tips in the stuff so that any hit that pierces the skin will be a deadly one.

**HOLMES:**  Am I correct when I say the poison causes apnea – the cessation of breath?

**REDVERS-G:**  You are correct, sir.

**HOLMES:**  Thank you, you have summoned up the cause of this man's death very succinctly.  Perhaps it is possible that you have brought some of this poison back home with you?

**REDVERS-G:**  I bring many native artefacts back but I do not have such poison.

**HOLMES:**  ( *appealing to the audience*) Has anybody here seen this velvet leaf poison in this country anywhere?

**SPECTATOR 1:**  I have!

**HOLMES:**  You, sir?  Where did you see it?

**SPECTATOR 1:**  When I went to play chess with Basil Redvers-Gordon.  He showed it to me in his library.

**HOLMES:**  What do you have to say to that, sir?

**REDVERS-G:**  I do not have any such poison now.  Perhaps it was some time ago when this gentlemen visited my house.

**HOLMES:**  So you did have some at one time?  What happened to it?

**REDVERS-G:**  I regret to say I do not know.

**HOLMES:**  That seems an unsatisfactory reply.  To be so careless with a deadly poison.

**REDVERS-G:**  You must understand, Mr Holmes, my house is a treasure trove of artefacts and wonders from all over the world.  After every expedition I bring back many

many things. None of these objects is catalogued and I have so much stuff I do not know the half of what I've got.

**HOLMES:** I see. Perhaps you would be so kind as to tell us why you took such an interest in the piano when you entered the room?

**REDVERS-G:** That is easily explained. A colleague of mine, who is resident in Africa, wishes me to arrange the delivery of a piano to him. As you must know the climate in the tropics is very hot and very humid. These are terrible conditions for a piano. I have said I am not a music lover. I was merely looking at the piano with an interest as to how it would survive both the climate and the shipping. That is all.

**HOLMES:** Thank you, you have been most co-operative.

**REDVERS-G:** I have no reason not to be.

**HOLMES:** Well Watson, we have a quandary. It would seem that nobody approached the piano except these two people. The leader of the musicians assures us that the piano was free of razor blades when he/she inspected it as the members were entering.

**WATSON:** Then, Holmes, one of the two must be the criminal.

**HOLMES:** Are you seriously suggesting that one man should kill another for the trivial reason that the funding for his expedition has been withdrawn? Or, that in the other case, Mr Morello has killed a rival through professional jealousy?

**WATSON:**   You of all people, Holmes, know that when a man broods on what he perceives to be an injustice he may be tempted to any kind of wickedness.

**REDVERS-G:**   I must correct you, Mr Holmes.  I do not regard the funding of my expedition as trivial. However I am thankful to say that the Royal Geographical Society has consented to make up the deficiency.  I shall be leaving tomorrow morning.

**HOLMES:**   Indeed?  You are to leave tomorrow morning yet you spend your last night before departure at a recital of a music society of which you are not even a member?  Come, sir.  You must have much more important matters to attend to.

**REDVERS-G:**   I see it is hopeless trying to fool you, Mr Holmes.  Very well.  I came to see a certain lady.  I am leaving this country for ever.  I do not intend to return ever again.  My heart has been broken.  I plan to spend the rest of my life buried in my work.

**HOLMES:**   I see; the real reason for your presence here is nothing to do with your funding difficulties but to say farewell to a certain lady?

**REDVERS-G:**   Not even that.  I did not hope to speak. Merely to take away a last vision of my beloved.

**CHAIRMAN:**   There are no unaccompanied ladies here tonight, sir.

**REDVERS-G:**   Oh, she is accompanied all right.  But I expected her to be with her new paramour, certainly not on the arm of Hudson Shawcross.

**NORMAN:**   Edmund, I thought you were a gentleman!

**REDVERS-G:**  And I thought you were a lady!

**HOLMES:**  These are deep waters.  You say you did not expect to see Miss Norman with Mr Shawcross.  With whom did you expect to see her?

**REDVERS-G:**  With Guido Salvato, the Gloved Pianist.

**HOLMES:**  Do you mean to say that Miss Norman broke off with you to have a liaison with the man who is now dead?

**REDVERS-G:**  She did.  I thought she loved me as passionately as I loved her but I was sadly mistaken. (*returning to his seat*) I cannot wait to leave the country.

**HOLMES:**  Have you anything to say to this, Miss Norman?

**NORMAN:**  Only that I thought I associated with gentlemen.

**HOLMES:**  Come, madam, I think we need to know a little more.

**NORMAN:**  What do you want me to say?  Yes, it's true that Edmund and I were lovers.  It's also true that he is the most boring man on earth. Every time I visited his home he showed me these trinkets and souvenirs that he had brought back from some God-awful place.

**HOLMES:**  These trinkets etc.  Did he ever show you a phial of poison from the Amazon?

**NORMAN:**  He might have.  I don't remember. (*pause*) There were so many things.

**HOLMES:**  Pray continue.

**NORMAN:**  Well he was always so serious. His idea of a good night out was to listen to a Christian missionary talk about converting the heathen in China.  A girl wants something a bit more exciting than that.

**HOLMES:**  So you took up with the Gloved Pianist?

**NORMAN:**  Yes.  He swept me off my feet.  I couldn't resist Guido's Italian charm.  He took me to Venice and Rome, the opera in Milan.  We went to Sicily to meet his family.  He introduced me to his brothers. We had a wonderful time.

**MORELLO:**  (*leaping to his feet*) So that's it!  All the time you were supposed to be with me you were two-timing with that – that – apology of a musician!

**NORMAN:**  Sit down, Aubrey, don't make a fool of yourself.  You are nothing in this.

**MORELLO:**  I?  Nothing?  I who have been reduced to poverty through lavishing gifts on you?  Nothing?

**NORMAN:**  I got you a job as rehearsal pianist for my next show, what more do you want?

**MORELLO:**  I will kill this woman!

Morello makes towards Norman.   Watson and Chairman hold him back.

**HOLMES:**  I am sure you have been sorely used Mr Morello.  But there has been serious violence done here tonight.  Do not add to it.

**MORELLO:**  I apologise.  (*sits down*)

**WATSON:**  Holmes, the tattoo – CN – Celia Norman!

**HOLMES:**  You think Salvato was so enamoured of Miss Norman he had the tattoo done as some kind of love token?

**WATSON:**  It is just the sort of thing a Latin gigolo would do.

**SHAWCROSS:**  Well, Miss Norman, it seems that I am at the end of quite a long line.

**NORMAN:**  Don't be silly, darling, you knew I wasn't exactly chaste.

**SHAWCROSS:**  Chased?  Chased?  It seems you've been chased and caught by half the fellows in London!

**NORMAN:**  They were mere peccadilloes, darling.  You know it is you whom I truly love.

**SHAWCROSS:**  Do I?  I think at the time you gave that impression to the other fellows too.

**NORMAN:**  Oh, darling, would I pretend to you?

**SHAWCROSS:**(*mollified*)  Well I suppose not.

**HOLMES:**  I think you can settle your affairs privately. I see, Watson, you have been taking notes.  Would you care to sum up the position?

**WATSON:**  Certainly, Holmes.  (*consults notes*)  We have four people involved in this death in some way.  Miss Celia Norman was the paramour of them all.  Mr Redvers-

Gordon has had his heart broken and is leaving the country.  Mr Morello has been reduced to poverty and cast aside.  Both these gentlemen were thrown over in favour of Guido Salvato the Gloved Pianist who is the murdered man. Mr Shawcross is her present beau.  We know Salvato met his death by the dastardly means of razor blades and poison.  We know both Redvers-Gordon and Morello had access to the piano.  Mr Shawcross is the manufacturer of these razor blades.  Mr Redvers-Gordon admits to having possessed a deadly poison of the type used.  Miss Norman could well have obtained possession of this poison unbeknownst to Mr Redvers-Gordon.  Mr Morello admits that he has had a life-long hatred for the dead man.

**HOLMES:**  Well done, Watson. In your usual inimitable manner you have honed directly in on the nub of the problem.  I am sure that more evidence will come to light.  If any of you have anything you wish to say in confidence to me or Dr Watson then please do not hesitate to speak to us.  Similarly, if you wish to discuss this awful case with each other, all to the good.  I am sure that together, before leaving the hall tonight, we will find the murderer.

There is a commotion at the back of the hall and a man rushes in and pushes his way to the front waving a telegram.

**NEWCOMER:**  Ladies and gentlemen, wonderful news! The Wright brothers have flown their flying machine in the air for over thirty minutes!

**CHAIRMAN:**  That is splendid news.  I think this would be a good time to break for supper.  It will be served immediately.

### END OF PART ONE

## SUPPER BREAK

During the supper break Holmes and Watson mingle and ask questions of the members of the audience and the suspects may also chat to people trying to throw suspicion off themselves on to one of the others.

Also raffle tickets may be sold, or, if sold before the play starts, the draw could take place. This is also the time that the judges may deliberate on choosing the best costume.

## PART TWO

The CHAIRMAN, SHAWCROSS and NORMAN step up on to the dais.

**CHAIRMAN:**  Please take your seats, ladies and gentlemen.  We are now going to award the prize for the best dressed lady and the best dressed gentleman.  We have had a judging committee comprising Dr Watson, Mr Hudson Shawcross and Miss Celia Norman.  In their opinion the lady winner is ???? and the gentleman winner is ????  Will those persons kindly come forward and Miss Norman will award them with their prizes.

SHAWCROSS and NORMAN stand with the prizes in their hands, the CHAIRMAN stands behind them as they present them to the two recipients.  Shawcross & Norman then sit.

**CHAIRMAN:**  The raffle has been drawn.  If you have a winning ticket please make your way to the raffle table at the end of the evening and collect your prize.  These are the winning numbers.(*reads out the winning numbers*)  I now call on Mr Sherlock Holmes to inform us of his deliberations.  Mr Holmes?

Holmes and Watson take their places on the rostrum.

**HOLMES:**  Well I am sure many of you have formed an opinion about who is the perpetrator of this heinous crime.  I have been making further investigations and I am sure you will be relieved to hear that I am confident that I have found the murderer.  I have been piecing all the known facts together like a jigsaw puzzle.  But there was one essential piece that eluded me.  You may be surprised to learn that seeing the prizes awarded tonight gave me that missing piece[7]. We have heard Mr Redvers-Gordon and Mr Morello explain their reasons for visiting the piano prior to the concert starting. Perhaps those reasons were not as innocent as they claim? We have also heard that a deadly South American poison was administered – a poison that Mr Redvers-Gordon freely admits he brought into this country. He then claims to have lost track of it. Miss Norman who carried on an illicit affaire with Mr Redvers-Gordon had ample opportunity to abstract the phial of poison on one of her many visits to Mr Redvers-Gordon's house. Miss Norman likes to give the impression she is a self-centred shallow lady who knows nothing apart from her world of the theatre. A world of frivolity and vanity. But the fact that she is able to string along one man after another shows she is cunning and deceitful. Men – like Mr Morello – whose emotions are so twisted by her they become desperate. And then we have Mr Shawcross who is an astute business man manufacturing under licence the latest invention – a safety razor blade. An ironic object seeing it brought the opposite of safety to poor Mr Salvato, the Gloved Pianist.

You may be interested to know, ladies and gentlemen, that I and Dr Watson between us interviewed every person in this hall during supper. I would be grateful if all the gentlemen present would humour me in this request – would those of you who in this year of our Lord 1905 have previously never heard of these so-called safety razor blades please raise your left hand.

All cast[8] except Holmes and Shawcross raise hands. All the males in the audience should too but it does not matter if they do not.

**SHAWCROSS:** But they will, Mr Holmes. By this time next year all the fellows will be using them.

**HOLMES:** I am sure you are right, Mr Shawcross. Thank you. Now would all the gentlemen who have read or heard about these blades raise their right hand. Thank you. So we come to the dénouement.

**CHAIRMAN:** Are you about to reveal a name to us, Mr Holmes?

**HOLMES:** I am, sir.

**CHAIRMAN:** Might I suggest a little game, sir?

**HOLMES:** Game, sir? We are talking about a murder, not playing games.

**CHAIRMAN:** Just a little vote, sir. Our members have been very patient and co-operative and many will have formed their own opinion of the murderer. It would be pleasant if they could tell their friends they were as – what was the word you just used – astute[9] as the great detective, Sherlock Holmes.

**WATSON:** What a vile suggestion!

**HOLMES:** Let him have his way, Watson

**CHAIRMAN:** Please raise your hand (*demonstrates*[10]) if you think Mr Hudson Shawcross is the guilty party. Those suspecting Mr Morello, those who think Mr Redvers-Gordon is the culprit. Those who suspect our guest of honour Miss Celia Norman. (*if there are several for her she can swoon*) Thank you. Pray proceed Mr Holmes.

**HOLMES:** There is one more suspect. Pray raise your hand if you suspect our worthy Chairman.

**CHAIRMAN:** Me, Mr Holmes? You surely jest?

**HOLMES:** Watson will tell you my sense of humour is rather limited. You pass yourself off as an Englishman but you are in fact an Italian. You have mastered the English language excellently yet there are lapses when you are agitated. Also you use Italian expressions when an Englishman would not. A true born Englishman would say 'open air' not 'al fresco'. You referred to an 'ambulanza' rather than an ambulance, 'Parigi' for Paris and so on. The word 'astute' was obviously unfamiliar to you as was the town of Folkestone which you pronounced in an incorrect manner. There were other examples.

**CHAIRMAN:** So I am not a true-born Englishman. I may have suffered in the lottery of life by not being born an Englishman but it is not yet a crime to be a foreigner to these shores.

**HOLMES:** No, your nationality is not a crime but in this country murder is, even if in your homeland such a thing is treated more casually.

**CHAIRMAN:** But how could I have done it? I went nowhere near the piano.

**HOLMES:** I confess that point puzzled me. Right up to the time of the prizegiving when you were hidden from view by your guests of honour. I then recalled you were in the very same position at the beginning of the evening when you introduced your guests to us. You were completely hidden for a full half minute while Miss Norman boosted her forthcoming musical comedy.

**NORMAN:** (*outraged*) Boost!?!

**HOLMES:** Ample time to place the razor blades in position. I am afraid, Watson, that you put rather a red herring in our way by suggesting that the tattoo on the wrist of Signor Salvato, the Gloved Pianist was a love token. When our worthy Chairman delighted us during the concert with his song (*or recitation*) which he rendered in such an over-blown theatrical manner, he exposed his left wrist. I observed his wrist carried the same tattoo. This I confirmed when he exposed it again recently during my request for the gentlemen to raise their hands.

**WATSON:**  So that's why you asked that? I thought it was pointless as any man could easily lie!

**HOLMES:**  How else could I contrive to see the man's wrist without arousing his suspicion? A simple subterfuge. The Chairman then kindly assisted in confirmation by once again raising his hand when he proposed the repugnant idea of voting on the identity of the murderer.

**WATSON:**  But what is the significance of the tattoos?

**HOLMES:**  The initials CN stand not for our guest of honour but for the Italian words Cosa Nostra. A secret society perhaps better known as the mafia. Salvato was obviously a member of the brotherhood – Miss Norman said she met his brothers in Sicily, the home of the Cosa Nostra. Salvato is a well-known Sicilian name. Salvato wore gloves so that the tattoo would not be revealed when he played the piano. Our Chairman is what is known as a 'hit-man'. He was sent by his masters to assassinate Salvato who had obviously transgressed in some way.

**CHAIRMAN:**  Curse you, Holmes! You'll never take me alive! (*he turns and flees through the door*)

**HOLMES:**  After him, Watson!

Watson chases out after him. The door is left open and

we hear the sound of London traffic.  The honking of a horn and the sound of a car braking, shouting, horses neighing.  Watson returns.

**WATSON:**   He was right Holmes, we will not take him alive.  He has cheated the gallows.  He ran straight out and tried to cross Baker Street.  He ran into a motor car that was just pulling up outside.  A Pierce Arrow tonneau.  The chauffeur didn't have a chance and the car ploughed into him.

**SHAWCROSS:**   That will be my car.  I ordered it for ten o'clock.

**HOLMES:**   Well, Watson.  Tonight has been unique in my experience – two deaths by means that would have been impossible just a few years ago.  Safety razor blades and a motor car.

**WATSON:**   Modern times, Holmes.

**HOLMES:**   Yes, Watson.  Modern methods but the same age-old lusts and passions.  Well, ladies and gentlemen, I regret your musical evening has been ruined but it is too late to continue now.  And as our Chairman cannot bring the proceedings to a close perhaps I can use a little of the Italian language when I quote the closing lines of Leoncavallo's famous opera "*I Pagliacci*" – "La commedia è finita!" – the play is over.  Good night.

Holmes & Watson bow.  The remainder of the cast file in.  Curtain call.

## THE END

# NOTES:

## I

The play is provided throughout with **ten** clues to the true murderer.  Most of these are indicated in Holmes's summing up.  Here is the complete list – the numbers coincide with the small superscript numbers in the play text.:

The Chairman has a tattoo identical to The Gloved Pianist on the inside of his left wrist.  This is *very briefly* exposed on three occasions:

(1)  when he is singing/reciting

(8)  when Holmes asks the men if they have heard of razor blades

(10)  when the Chairman himself indicates how the audience should raise their hand when voting.

On several occasions the Chairman lapses into Italian words.  These are: *al fresco***(2)**, *mamma mia***(4)**, *ambulanza***(5)**.  He also pronounces Folkestone**(3)** incorrectly and names Paris in the Italian form of Parigi**(6)**.  He does not know the word *astute*.**(9)**

Holmes in his summary after supper says: "However there was one essential piece missing from the jigsaw.  Seeing the prizes awarded tonight gave me that missing piece." **(7)**  Which is when he realises that the Chairman was concealed by the standing guests of honour in an identical manner to when they were first introduced.

## II

The play may be presented to an audience conventionally seated theatre-style, the audience leaving to another room for supper.  It is preferable to be staged cabaret-style with the audience arranged at tables round three sides of the room with the 'bandstand' at the fourth side or in a corner. In this case the supper is served to them at the tables. In either layout the seats for the actors in the play must be conveniently located so that when they have to rise or leave those seats the way is not impeded. Thus those seats have 'reserved' cards placed on them prior to the doors opening.

### III

At two points in the play two EXTRA CHARACTERS are briefly brought in – A SPECTATOR and a NEWCOMER. These can be played by the same person and if an actor is not available two suitable members of the audience may be primed as they enter. In this case it would be wise to have their brief lines printed on a postcard.

### IV

Although such entertainments as this are known as 'Murder Mystery Evenings' it would be wise not to use the word 'murder' in any pre-publicity. The recommended formula being SHERLOCK HOLMES MYSTERY EVENING.

# NOTICE

Lightning Source UK Ltd.
Milton Keynes UK
UKHW011643190821
389122UK00002B/650